He Came to Her from Far Away . . .
and Promised Her Forever . . .

Tabitha looked up at Tom. His white-blonde hair was blowing back from his forehead. "Are you going with the *White Swan* when she sails again?" she asked.

Tom nodded. "If your father'll have me as a hand."

Tabitha's heart beat with excitement. If her father agreed to take her with him on his next trip, she and Tom would go sailing off together, away from stuffy little New Bedford. They would see the golden coast of California and the exotic ports of China.

She turned to Tom, her eyes shining. She longed to tell him of her plan to sail on the *White Swan* . . .

"Tabitha," Tom said, as if he were able to read her thoughts. "Tabitha—" He bent down and his lips brushed very lightly against hers. Then she was in his arms and he was kissing her.

Tabitha closed her eyes and felt her body lean into his, as if it had a mind of its own . . .

Dawn of Love

PROMISE FOREVER

Dee Austin

AN ARCHWAY PAPERBACK
Published by POCKET BOOKS • NEW YORK

AN ARCHWAY PAPERBACK *Original*

An Archway Paperback published by
POCKET BOOKS, a division of Simon & Schuster, Inc.
1230 Avenue of the Americas, New York, N.Y. 10020

ISBN: 0-671-55156-6

First Archway Paperback printing October, 1985

10 9 8 7 6 5 4 3 2 1

Printed in the U.S.A.

IL 7+

PROMISE FOREVER

Chapter 1

TABITHA WALKER PACED BACK AND FORTH ON THE narrow porch that wound its way around the upper story of the white-shingled house.

She paused and looked toward the busy port of New Bedford, Massachusetts. She saw the same ships at anchor that she had seen just five minutes before, and she saw no new sails along the horizon.

Tabitha resumed her walking on the narrow slat boards that she liked to call "the upstairs porch." Everyone else in New Bedford called such a walkway a "widow's walk," because of the many women who had stood there, staring out to sea, hoping to catch a glimpse of ships and men that were fated never to return to their home port.

Tabitha hated that name, hated the very idea of a widow's walk. In her own life it had been her mother, not her father, who'd died first. And now her father, far out to sea captaining his ship, the *White Swan*, sailed on without her.

What rankled Tabitha was that she—*she*—was left on shore to watch and wait, to hear bright, mouthwatering snatches of what the rest of the world was like. Sixteen was old enough to go to sea, she reasoned impatiently. Her mother had sailed at eighteen as her father's bride. And sixteen wasn't that different from eighteen now, was it?

A fresh, vibrant breeze blew against her cheek. It rocked the anchored ships and filled her chest with a longing to see the world, to sail to all the mysterious places that, now, were only words to her, to find the magic spring that would set her life in motion.

"Tabitha," she heard her uncle call from the parlor below. She chose to ignore him, but she couldn't ignore the pounding noise he made as he thumped the ceiling with his silver-headed cane. "*Tabitha!*"

Tabitha sighed, stepped back into her bedroom and ran down the narrow wooden stairs to the kitchen.

"Tabitha," Uncle Silas said in his flint-and-granite New Bedford voice, shaking his head at Tabitha's wind-tangled hair, "the *White Swan* isn't due back for a week or more. No sense your standing up there craning your neck like a goose. Your aunt needs your help down here."

Aunt Priscilla looked up from the large bowl of green apples she was peeling for a pie. She knew how Tabitha felt about working in the kitchen, knew how little she liked cooking.

"Too many cooks spoil the broth," Aunt Priscilla said kindly, and Tabitha felt a wave of relief. "Didn't you say you could use some help with the accounts, Silas? Tabitha would probably be a lot more use at the store."

"Come on then, Tabitha." Uncle Silas didn't have any trouble making his mind up, once Aunt Priscilla showed him the way. "You can make out some bills for me—your writing's good and clear."

"Thank you, Aunt Priss," Tabitha said, and bent to give her aunt's cheek a quick peck. She would have been out the door in another minute if Priscilla Byrd hadn't stopped her.

"Not like that, Tabitha," her aunt said, her lips puckering like dried-up apple. "Brush your hair back, put on a bonnet, and take a parasol."

Tabitha's foot tapped restlessly. She wanted to say that the store was only three short streets away—hardly a walk that needed a bonnet and a parasol—but she thought better of it and decided not to argue. Aunt Priscilla was smooth as honey when you went her way, but contradict her too often and she got as stirred up as a hornet's nest.

Tabitha ran upstairs and brushed back her long, dark red hair with three quick swipes of a brush. She thought of tying it neatly with one of the silk ribbons her father had brought her from China, but she was too impatient, so she pushed her hair back behind her ears and tied a straw bonnet beneath her chin. The bonnet tilted to one side, but Tabitha didn't take time to straighten it.

Parasol. Aunt Priscilla had said parasol, but where *was* her parasol? She couldn't find the little flowered sun umbrella that her aunt would approve of, but she did find the large, waxed-paper one that her father had brought from China along with the ribbons. It had a shiny red-laçquered handle that Tabitha loved, and with this parasol in hand she ran down the stairs again.

Priscilla looked up from her apple bowl as Tabitha whirled before her. Her hair was neat—well, as neat as that mass of bright auburn hair could ever be—and the pale green dress didn't seem too crushed, not when you considered that Tabitha had worn it while climbing a tree to rescue Canton, the cat. But that umbrella—that umbrella!

"Tabitha," Aunt Priscilla called out as her niece was about to sail through the open door. She put the bowl on the kitchen table and went to the door. "If you can't find a proper parasol, use one of mine."

Uncle Silas paused and looked at the shiny paper umbrella that Tabitha held above her head. He snorted with laughter and called back to his wife, "That's what happens when your family is in the China trade, Priscilla. Besides, it's good Yankee sense to make use of what you own."

Priscilla Byrd shook her head and went back into the kitchen. It was hard bringing up a child, especially a girl—and especially a girl who was your niece, not your own daughter.

Tabitha walked beside her uncle until they reached the cobblestoned street that faced the harbor. As usual, Uncle Silas stopped to admire the gold-lettered sign above the entrance:

Byrd & Walker
Shipping Supplies, Imported Goods
Founded 1820

"That's us," Tabitha said, twirling the red-lacquered handle of the umbrella. Uncle Silas, the Byrd of Byrd & Walker, nodded. In her father's absence, Tabitha proudly considered herself the Walker. It made her feel important—in touch, somehow, with the world that shimmered just beyond the harbor.

Uncle Silas opened the front door with a large metal key and Tabitha followed him into the store. She loved the smell of the place and the way it looked, full of coils of rope and bolts of canvas on one side and, on the other, canisters of tea, jars of spices, and bolts of cloth. Tabitha took a deep breath—you could smell the sea when you were in Byrd & Walker's.

She followed her uncle to a corner of the store where there was a slanted writing table with a tall stool in front of it. Tabitha perched on the stool while Uncle Silas rummaged in a drawer for a bunch of papers that were scrawled with items and numbers. Hopefully, Tabitha could read them and turn them into proper bills. As she readied a pot of ink and a pen and some nibs, she asked her uncle a question that had only recently occurred to her, "How did you and Papa decide who would go to sea and who would manage the business in New Bedford?"

Uncle Silas shook his head. "No trouble deciding that. Your father, Jedediah, liked the sea. I was always a homebody. And after I married Jedediah's sister—your Aunt Priscilla—it seemed right smart for us to form a company with each one doing what he liked best. It's been twenty years, Tabitha, and I don't think either one of us has regretted it."

Tabitha nodded and bent over the papers, her mind working as busily as the square-faced clock on the wall. It must be in the blood, then, she decided, this whole business of wanting to go to sea. First her father had gone, and her mother with him. So it was no wonder that their daughter should feel the same way. For Tabitha did want to go to sea, wanted to go so badly she could almost taste the salty air in her mouth.

If I were a boy, Tabitha thought as she eyed the pile of papers before her, *if I were a boy I would have sailed two years ago.*

Fourteen. That was the age for New Bedford boys to decide whether they'd be sailors or not. But girls had no such choices. It was so unfair that Tabitha shook several drops of black ink from the tip of her pen in spite.

The clock chimed, reminding her that she had accounts to tally. But before she started working on them, she counted once again the years since she'd last seen her father. Four years—four whole years—that's how long he had been away. She loved her aunt and uncle, of course. They were kind and caring, but she missed her father, and ever since her mother had died five years ago, she missed him even more. Aunts and uncles were fine, but Jedediah Walker was her father—he was the one she wanted to be with, sailing over the wide sea in the *White Swan,* just as her mother had once done.

Tabitha started working on the bills, but every now and then she looked up from the desk to see her uncle happily bustling about the store. The ships' supplies were in good order, but he was making room for the goods he was expecting—the goods that Jedediah Walker was bringing back from China.

There would be the white porcelain dishes decorated with blue willow trees, bolts of gleaming silks—crimson, peacock blue, emerald green—and cases of teas that held the flavor and aroma of mysterious lands to the east. All those things came from China, and there would be packets of furs as well—sea otter skins from off the coast of California. These would all become part of the Byrd & Walker stores.

And, of course, Captain Jedediah Walker would also bring gifts: something special for his daughter, Tabitha was sure of that, and items both lovely and useful for his sister and brother-in-law.

But now that she was sixteen, Tabitha didn't care all that much about the presents her father would bring her—she cared about *him*, seeing him and hearing the thrilling stories he brought back to her. Tabitha understood that her father would always be a sea captain, just as her uncle would always be a merchant, but she was a sea captain's daughter—she wanted to see for herself what the world was made of. And make no mistake about it, she was going to. Tabitha made up her mind—the next time the *White Swan* left port, she meant to be on it.

And that was what Tabitha told her aunt and uncle that evening as they were finishing the last of their hot apple pie, which had been generously slathered with clabbered cream.

Aunt Priscilla smiled, but Uncle Silas burst out laughing when he heard what Tabitha said. "A girl aboard the *White Swan!* The day that happens I guess half the sailors will jump ship."

"Why?" Tabitha asked indignantly. "My mother sailed on the *White Swan.*"

"Your mother was a sea captain's wife," Aunt Priscilla explained, "and some captains' wives do sail with their husbands—though your mother never sailed with your father after you were born."

"Well," Tabitha said, "I'm a captain's daughter—why can't I sail with my father?"

Aunt Priscilla looked at Tabitha across the table. She had thought of her niece as a little girl, but she could see that this past year had made her into a young woman. That flow of silky auburn hair framed a heart-shaped face in which dark blue eyes sparkled like jewels. And Tabitha had shot up so! She was tall but delicately curved, like the fine-rigged schooners that bobbed impatiently along the wharf.

"Why can't I sail with my father?" Tabitha repeated impatiently.

Because you'll stir up nothing but fights among those sailor lads, Priscilla Byrd wanted to say, but didn't. No sense telling Tabitha how much power she had over the half of the world that was male—she'd find that out for herself soon enough.

"Because young ladies don't go to sea," Priscilla said at last. "They just don't."

For a fleeting minute, Priscilla Byrd wondered if she and Silas had done all they should have for their niece.

Would Tabitha's mother, if she had lived, have seen to it that Tabitha had more of a social life? No wonder the girl talked of sailing away from New Bedford! They hadn't done enough to keep her happy here. Priscilla determined to do something about that the very next day—perhaps invite some young people for afternoon tea.

She thought about this as she and Tabitha cleared the dining room table. The problem was, who was there to invite? Oh, there were plenty of young girls Tabitha's age, but there were very few boys. Most of the young men of New Bedford went to sea, and Priscilla didn't know too many families who weren't part of the New Bedford merchant fleet.

But never mind, where there was a will there was a way, that's what she had been brought up to believe, and she was determined to get Tabitha's mind off sailing on the *White Swan*.

She smiled to herself. The idea! A girl on a sailing ship. Not that Jedediah would ever permit it. Priscilla felt easier. If she and Silas couldn't get their niece to forget the idea, she was sure that Jedediah could. As they washed up, Priscilla tried to remember the names of some cousins living around Boston way. She would write to them the very next morning and see if she couldn't arrange an invitation for Tabitha.

A trip to Boston—that would be exciting, that would take Tabitha's mind off going to sea. Priscilla Byrd smiled, certain she knew her niece's mind.

* * *

The next morning, Priscilla sat down before the small walnut desk in her bedroom and started to compose a letter. It wasn't easy—she hadn't heard from her cousins in years—but still, they were kin.

She was well into the second paragraph, explaining that Tabitha was a second cousin once removed, when she heard Tabitha's shout from the widow's walk above.

"Tabitha," Priscilla called as she ran to the window, the letter forgotten, "what is it? What's the matter?"

"The *White Swan,*" Tabitha shouted. "I see it—she's come home."

"Can't be," Priscilla called up to Tabitha, "Silas said it wasn't due for a week or more."

"They must have had good trade winds," said Tabitha, "because I see her—it is the *White Swan.*"

Priscilla pulled her head back in, closed the window, and ran up the stairs. She came out to the widow's walk where Tabitha stood, and looked out to sea. There was a ship, she could see that, but from such a distance she wasn't at all sure that it was the *White Swan*.

"How can you tell?" she asked her niece. "How do you know it's the *White Swan?*"

"The figurehead," Tabitha said impatiently. "Can't you see it, Aunt Priss? The body of a mermaid, with the wings and neck of a white swan. Can't you see it?"

Priscilla Byrd couldn't quite make out the figurehead that decorated the bow of the ship. It was still too far away, and she hoped that her niece was not going to be disappointed. She looked at Tabitha—her dark red hair blowing in the wind, her eyes shining with happiness. Why the child was beautiful! Strange how she had never really noticed it before last night. Tabitha looked like one of those sculptured figureheads herself.

She remained beside her niece until the ship came closer, her sails still billowed out by a wind that had brought her home earlier than expected. The captain of that ship certainly sailed his vessel the way her brother did. Jedediah always did love to come into port with a fast wind behind him, not shortening sail until the very last minute, until it looked as though the wind would deposit him right on their doorstep.

"Aunt Priss—"

Priscilla shaded her eyes from the sun. "I think—yes, I do think—"

"It *is*, Aunt Priss—it is!"

Priscilla hugged Tabitha to her and laughed. "You're right, Tabitha. It's the *White Swan*, come home to us after four years!"

The two hugged each other again and then hurried from the widow's walk back into the house. They were on their way to the wharves to watch the *White Swan* anchor, and they wouldn't be alone there. The families of the men on board were also hurrying to the port, as were those who hoped that the *White Swan* brought mail and messages from other New Bedford sailing vessels.

No matter how often a sailing ship came into port it was a great occasion. The women and children knew that not all sailing vessels returned home—many were lost at sea—and anytime a ship put into port it was a day of happiness and excitement.

They were halfway to port when Priscilla thought to say, "Oh, Tabitha, you're not wearing a bonnet."

Tabitha laughed, and reached out for her aunt's hand. "No, Aunt Priss," she said, "and neither are you!"

Priscilla Byrd reached up and smoothed back her hair, dark brown streaked with gray. "I guess we can be forgiven—it doesn't happen very often."

"Once in four years," Tabitha laughed as they hurried along.

"That's right," her aunt echoed, "once in four years."

Chapter 2

WHEN TABITHA AND HER AUNT REACHED THE WHARF they joined Silas, who had left his shop to welcome the *White Swan*.

"It's beautiful," Tabitha said, as she watched the sailing ship tack to the right, and then shorten sail.

"Here he comes," Silas whooped, "and he's coming fast—liable to pile right up against the dock."

"Don't worry, Uncle Silas," Tabitha said, sure of her father's skills. "Papa will do just fine!"

Make me proud, Tabitha thought, *show them what kind of a captain you are, Papa.* And she beamed when the sailing ship slowed at just the right moment and slid neatly up to the wharf, gliding over the water as easily as a skater gliding on a pond's frozen surface of ice.

A crowd of people had gathered, and there were cheers and shouts and waves as everyone crowded about, eager to welcome the homecoming crew.

"Do you see him?" Tabitha asked her aunt. "Do you see my father?"

"Not yet," Priscilla said, "but he's got lots to do,

Tabitha—the ship isn't even tied up yet. Give him a minute or two, child."

"A minute or two!" Tabitha exclaimed. "After four years?" Waiting. She was waiting again, while her father and all the other men aboard the *White Swan* had something to do. Her heart thumped anxiously in her chest and she tossed her head in the sharp, salty air. As Tabitha watched with her aunt and uncle, members of the crew came up to the ship's railing and waved to the people below.

"Have you seen the whaler *Blue Sky?"* a woman with a child tugging at her skirts called to the men on the ship. "Anybody seen the whaler *Blue Sky?"*

"Saw the *Blue Sky* in the Falkland Islands, ma'am," a sailor shouted to her. "Should be coming along in a week or two."

The woman waved and smiled. "Thank you," she said, "thank you. It's been three years," she said to the Byrds and Tabitha as she stopped by their side, "three years since I saw my man." She pointed to her child. "When he left this one was only two months old. He'll be surprised to see her so grown."

"Sure will," Priscilla said. "Just like Tabitha here. I can hardly wait for my brother to see his daughter."

The woman smiled at Tabitha. "Such a grown-up young lady. Do you think your father will recognize you?"

Tabitha's blue eyes stung the woman. "Of course he will," she said firmly. "Oh, look, Aunt Priss, the gangplank is down! Can we go on board?"

"You go ahead," Priscilla Byrd said. "Your uncle and I will wait here."

Tabitha ran over to the ship. Impatiently she squeezed among the sailors who were crowding down the narrow wooden plank that stretched from the ship to the wharf. She bobbed among them like a cork, jerking her dress free and pushing past them until, at last, she stood on the *White Swan's* deck. A round-faced seaman beamed a curious grin at her. "Well, missy, looks like you've got a sweetheart on the *White Swan* you're mighty eager to see."

The sailors standing near them laughed, and Tabitha flushed. "It's my father," she said. "I want to see my father."

"Your father, is it? And what would his name be? I didn't ship out with anyone handsome enough to have a daughter like you."

"His name is Jedediah Walker," Tabitha said proudly, advancing a step and enjoying the feeling of the smooth, straight planks of the *White Swan's* deck beneath her feet, "*Captain* Jedediah Walker." She smiled, her eyes lighting up like blue glass lanterns.

"Captain Walker? Stand back, now, it's the captain's daughter." The round-faced man grinned, surveying Tabitha's shapely figure. "The tiny mite of a girl he's told us of so often."

"Well," Tabitha admitted, "I guess I've grown some since he left." She glanced anxiously about the deck, aware that the sailors' eyes were on her. "Where *is* my father?" she asked the round-faced man.

"Below, missy," he told her. "One of the crew had an accident during the last storm, and the captain's just seeing to him."

"I'm going down to him," Tabitha said. She smiled jauntily at the round-faced man. "Don't worry, I can find my way—I was practically *born* on this ship, you know."

"Best to wait here, missy. It's a bit of a mess below, end of the voyage and all. I'll tell your father to come right up."

The man was gone before Tabitha could say that she wanted to go below with him, but it was only another minute or so before she heard a familiar voice. "What's the emergency, Plum? Just why do I have to go up on deck right away?"

Tabitha didn't hear Plum's reply, but suddenly a tall man emerged from below deck. He was thin and straight, and Tabitha felt a pang when she saw the streaks of gray in hair that she remembered as being glossy black. He was wearing a dark navy blue coat, the brass buttons sadly tarnished and, as she watched, he put his captain's hat firmly on the back of his head.

"Well?" he asked Plum impatiently. "What was all the hurry about?"

Plum pointed to where Tabitha stood. The breeze that had brought the *White Swan* home early blew her hair suddenly across her face, hiding her features. Her skirt billowed out too, outlining her slim figure.

Captain Walker blinked, the sun in his eyes, and though he saw the young woman standing before him, he couldn't see her face. She was tall—the wife of one of his crew members, no doubt, though why Plum had to hurry him on deck because of that, he didn't know.

Yet there was something familiar about her, and the captain walked slowly toward her. Then she lifted her hand, caught her billowing hair, and brushed it away from her face. "Tabitha!" Captain Walker exclaimed, hardly able to believe that this was the twelve-year-old child he had left behind. "My Tabitha—"

"Papa!" Tabitha cried as she skimmed across the last few feet that separated them, and then she was in her father's arms. "Oh, Papa!"

After a long embrace, Captain Walker held his daughter away from him and took a long look at her. He shook his head. "You're a beautiful young girl, no, a beautiful young *woman* and I—I've been away too long." He gave her another quick hug. "Looks like I've missed all your growing up years."

"You didn't miss much," Tabitha said with a quick laugh. "Oh, Papa, I've missed you so much, and the *White Swan* too."

And as her father went on about how tall she was, how pretty she had become, how much she reminded him of her mother, Tabitha thought with delight of her plans to go to sea. The *White Swan's* deck felt better than gold beneath her feet.

Minutes passed before Tabitha remembered that her aunt and uncle were waiting on the wharf below. "Papa, Aunt Priscilla and Uncle Silas must be wondering what happened to me."

"Of course," Jedediah Walker said, giving his daughter one more hug. "I've forgotten all about them." He frowned slightly, and said, "I'll go down and see them, but then I've got to come back to the *White Swan—*"

Tabitha took his arm. "Papa," she asked eagerly, "are you sailing away again? Sailing right away?"

"No, no, Daughter, nothing like that. I've got a hurt man below—he injured his knee during a storm. He's not from New Bedford and doesn't know anyone here in port. I can't leave him on the ship with no one but the men on watch. It wouldn't be right."

"But, Papa . . ." Tabitha felt a pang of disappointment. "I've been waiting for you for so long—we're all expecting you at the house. . . ."

Captain Walker thought for a minute. "Tabitha, go talk to your aunt and uncle. Ask them about my bringing this sailor home for a few days. He isn't hurt too badly—wouldn't really cause too much trouble."

Tabitha flew to where her aunt and uncle were waiting on the wharf. She quickly told them that her father was just fine, but that he had an injured sailor on board the *White Swan* with no place to go.

"Can we bring him home, Aunt Priss, Uncle Silas? Papa said he can't leave him on the ship all alone."

"Well, I don't know," Uncle Silas said slowly.

"Of course we can," Aunt Priscilla said. "If that's the only way we can get Jedediah off that ship, we'll do it. Silas and I will go home and fix up the spare room for the poor man. You go and tell Jedediah that everything's arranged, Tabitha. And then hurry home with him ever as fast as you can—I haven't seen my brother for four long years."

"Yes, you do that," Uncle Silas agreed, happy that his wife had taken the responsibility for making the decision. "Tell Jedediah that we're waiting for him."

Tabitha ran back up the gangplank, and round-faced Plum greeted her with a smile. "Captain's below, missy," he told her. "The cabin's right at the foot of those stairs there."

"I know where it is," Tabitha answered as she hurried down the stairs and into her father's cabin. There was a white-haired man lying on the captain's bunk, and Tabitha was prepared to see an old sailor, someone frail, with sunken cheeks and a stubbled beard.

"Tabitha," her father said, "this is Tom Howard."

The man on the bunk turned his head to greet Tabitha, and she saw that what she had taken for white hair was really burnished white gold, streaked even lighter in places by the sun.

Tom Howard propped himself up in the bunk. He was wearing one of her father's night shirts, but he was more broad-shouldered than Captain Walker and the shirt was open halfway down his chest. Tabitha found herself staring at the curly golden hairs that peeped through the open shirt front.

Tom Howard was young, probably only two or three years older than she herself was. And he was looking at her with bright, friendly eyes.

"Tom," Captain Walker said, "this is my daughter, Miss Tabitha Walker."

"Pleased to meet you, Miss Walker," Tom Howard said. His gray-green eyes sparkled with appreciation as he looked at Tabitha. "Real nice of you and your family to take an interest in me."

Did Tabitha imagine that his voice stressed the word *interest?* Or that the pupils of his eyes seemed to widen just a little when he looked at her?

"Did you talk to your aunt and uncle, Tabitha?" her father asked, breaking in on her thoughts. "Is it all right if Tom comes and spends a few days?"

"Just until my knee heals," Tom said quickly. "Don't want to be a burden."

"No burden," Tabitha said. Her voice sounded short and clipped. Almost breathless. But that was ridiculous, she told herself. Just because Tom Howard was handsome as a god . . .

"Are you sure?" Tom asked, studying Tabitha's face until she felt twin spots of color flame in her cheeks. *Darn* him, anyway, for making her feel so.

"We Yankees aren't given to gush," Captain Walker said, smiling at his daughter, "but if Tabitha says it's all right, then you can be sure it is all right."

Tom smiled. His smile, lighting his gray-green eyes, reminded Tabitha of a warm sunlit day at sea. She wanted a minute or two to think about that smile all by herself.

Tabitha turned away from the young man lying on the bunk and looked at her father. "Papa," she said, doing her best to hide her confusion, "how're we going to get Mr. Howard to the house?"

"Call me Tom, Miss Tabitha," he said, even as her father was explaining that there were still some members of his crew around, and that they'd be happy to lend a hand.

Tabitha trailed after her father when he left his cabin, and for a few minutes she saw him as the captain of the ship—the man in charge. His orders were quick and crisp: a few men had to stand watch even while the ship was in port, but they would be relieved in eight hours. Two other crewmen were ordered to rig a pallet for Tom and to carry him to the Byrd house.

"Come, Daughter," Captain Walker said, "we'll walk home. *Home*. It's good to say that word, and it's good to be in New Bedford again. We have a lot of catching up to do, Tabitha. You can tell me about New Bedford, and I'll tell you about China."

Tabitha and her father were strolling so slowly that the men carrying Tom actually passed them by. The men moved gingerly over the cobblestoned streets, but even though they were bouncing and jouncing Tom, he managed a wave and smile for Tabitha as they passed by.

That smile. Tabitha shook her head, and scolded herself silently. She had been eagerly waiting for her father, and she was sure that when they finally met after so many years she would hang on his every word. But meeting Tom Howard had made her lose track of what Jedediah Walker was saying.

"And after California, Papa?" she asked, trying to cover up the fact that she hadn't been listening. "Is that when you went to China?"

"No, Tabitha," Captain Walker said, "I just told you—after California we sailed to Hawaii. It was after Hawaii that we sailed to China."

"Of course, Papa," Tabitha said, biting her lip. "I'm just so happy to see you that I don't know what I'm saying."

"Don't worry about it, Daughter, we'll have plenty of time together for you to hear my sailor's yarns."

They had arrived at the white-shingled Byrd house, and Priscilla ran out of the house and threw her arms around her brother.

"Jedediah," she was crying, "Jedediah—it's been so long . . ."

Silas Byrd was beside his wife, and though he shook his brother-in-law's hand warmly, all he said was, "Good to see you, Jedediah," as though they had seen each other only yesterday.

Tabitha thought about what her father had said about all the time they would have together. But they would have a lot more time than he knew; when Captain Jedediah Walker left New Bedford again she was leaving with him!

Chapter 3

THE NEXT FEW DAYS WERE AMONG THE MOST EXCITING that Tabitha had ever known. Her emotions were a constant tangle, like one of Aunt Priscilla's yarn balls after Canton had gone after it.

Tom Howard was part of it, of course—no doubt about *that*. He could make her smile or, just as easily, fill her with sudden confusion. Tabitha lived in a constant state of expectation, her blood thumping just below the surface of her creamy skin.

But Tom Howard wasn't all that filled her mind. There was also her father, with his thrilling talk of the sea. If Captain Walker had known the effect his stories were having on his daughter, no doubt he would have tamed them a little. But he didn't know, and Tabitha's yearning to escape New Bedford only grew stronger and more insistent with each new tale.

Would Tom Howard sail with the *White Swan* again? That was the question Tabitha could not help wondering about, though she kept herself from asking her father for the answer. She didn't want anyone guessing how curious she was about Tom. Not yet.

But how could she help but be curious? she asked

herself. Without a doubt, Tom Howard was the most unusual boy she had ever known.

First of all, he was a runaway! Four years ago, when he was fifteen, he'd quarreled with his father—he didn't say about what—and signed on to a whaling ship that sailed out of Gloucester, Massachusetts. The ship had put in to the Falkland Islands for lengthy repairs, and it was there that Tom left the whaler, and joined the crew of the *White Swan*.

"What did the whaler's captain say about that?" asked Tabitha, who knew something about desertion and the rules of the sea.

"Well, it was all right with him," Tom admitted with a sheepish grin. "I was too inexperienced a hand to be much good on a whaler. I owe your father a lot, Tabitha. If I ever become a halfway good sailor it'll be because of him."

Tabitha. A shiver ran across her shoulders when he said her name. Of course they would call each other by their first names—Tabitha could see the sense in that. It would be silly for him to go around calling her Miss Walker. But still, the *way* he said her name made her look up at him, only to find his sea-colored eyes resting lightly on her.

Maybe it was silly, finding so much meaning in the use of a name. But she couldn't help it. She had never spent much time around boys, and lately almost none at all, now that all the boys her own age were away at sea. And there had never—ever—been a young man staying at the Byrd house before.

"So if I'm silly, well then, I'm silly, and that's all

there is to it," Tabitha told Canton, nudging him aside with her foot as she started up the stairs with Tom's breakfast tray.

The other thing that made Tom so different was that he was from the state of New York and the city of New York! All the people that Tabitha knew were from Massachusetts. Mostly, they were from New Bedford. She had met a few people from Boston and thereabouts, but she'd never met anyone from New York State, and she had certainly never met anyone from New York City.

"Oh, land, what's the difference where the boy is from?" Aunt Priscilla had asked impatiently when Tabitha tried to explain how she felt. "We're all Americans, aren't we? I guess people from New York are just as good as the people from Massachusetts." She paused. "Well, almost as good, anyway."

It wasn't a question of being as good, Tabitha thought, it was a question of being *different*. Different things had always delighted her, and Tom Howard was a different sort of person. Maybe he was only three years older than she was, but he seemed to know so much more, to have done so much more.

Well, of course, there was a reason for that, Tabitha thought with frustration. Tom had gone sailing halfway around the world—and aboard her own father's ship, too!—while all she had done was sit at home in boring New Bedford! It wasn't fair. But never mind, she thought, as she knocked on the door of Tom's room. Never mind. She was going to fix all that. Soon.

* * *

While Captain Walker and the *White Swan* were in port, neither man nor ship were on complete vacation. Jedediah Walker arranged for repairs on his ship, and talked to Silas Byrd about financial matters.

The *White Swan* had brought a cargo of silks, teas, porcelains, and furs, and Jedediah had to tell his brother-in-law what he had paid for the goods so that Silas could know what to charge for them when he sold them in his store.

Some days Tabitha went to the shop with her father and her uncle, and they kept her busy entering figures in the big, leather-covered ledger. But even at the store, her head filled with figures, she found herself thinking of Tom. What was he doing now? Was he thinking of some girl he'd known, a girl he'd called by her first name and maybe even kissed? Probably, Tabitha warned herself. He was probably thinking just that. After all, just because she hadn't known other boys didn't mean Tom Howard hadn't known other girls.

When Tabitha wasn't needed at the store she stayed home and helped Aunt Priscilla, who was determined to cook every single dish that she could remember her brother liking.

"Indian pudding," she declared one morning when Tabitha was barely awake. "Jedediah always loved it—we'll have it tonight. And steak and kidney pie, too."

Tabitha rolled her eyes. When Aunt Priscilla began her day with declarations like that it meant that she'd be trapped in the kitchen all day helping to prepare dinner.

Of course, she had to admit to herself that there was a bright spot: a day spent at home also meant a day when she saw more of Tom and his smile.

Indian Pudding Day. That's how Tabitha would always think of that day forever after—like a day marked on a calendar with special red letters. Of course, it wasn't the Indian pudding that made it special—it was Tom Howard.

It all began when she knocked on Tom's door, the breakfast tray carefully balanced in one hand.

"Come on in, Tabitha," she heard Tom say.

Tabitha opened the door, and the tray almost dropped from her hands when she saw him. Tom was dressed and standing beside the bed, and he was so tall!

For days she had admired Tom's smile and his eyes, which went from gray to green depending on his mood, but she had no real idea of how he looked until she saw him standing there before her. His shoulders were broad, he was lean, and she realized again that he was very good-looking. He was more than good-looking, in fact. With his sun-whitened hair and richly tanned skin, he was—well, handsome! New Bedford had nothing to compare to Tom Howard.

"Is your knee better?" she asked when she finally managed to say something.

"Thanks to you and all that good nursing care," he said, smiling.

Tabitha shook her head. "I didn't do any nursing."

"Carrying trays up and downstairs was plenty of nursing," Tom said. "My knee would never have healed if I'd had to walk on my bad leg." He had been holding on to one of the tall posts of the four-poster bed, and now he took a small step forward.

"I'm not sure," Tom said, and he swayed slightly. "I'm not sure if I've got my land legs back just yet."

Tabitha put the breakfast tray on the dresser and moved quickly to his side. "Here," she said, "lean on me. Your first day out of bed you've got to be careful."

The moment his arm went around her shoulders, Tabitha felt something . . . something warm and scary at the same time.

"Lucky you're tall, Tabitha," Tom said as they moved slowly toward the door. "It makes walking a lot easier." They took another step, and he said, "Lucky . . . and kind of nice, too."

Was the arm she felt around her shoulders holding her a little closer than necessary? Tabitha wasn't sure, but when she tried to edge away just a tiny bit from Tom, he almost stumbled again, so he leaned on her even more heavily.

Don't be silly, Tabitha warned herself silently. She was just helping a boy who had gotten hurt on her father's ship. There was no more to it than that. But Tabitha decided that she liked having Tom's arm around her shoulders nevertheless.

When they reached the door of the room, Tabitha asked, "Do you want to try making it downstairs,

Tom? Or do you think that'll be too much for your first day out of bed?"

Tom shook his head. "Won't be too much at all. Of course I'm going downstairs. I don't want to spend all my leave in one room. I want to see New Bedford—I've never been here before."

They started down the stairs very slowly. "Not much to see in New Bedford," Tabitha told him. "You probably saw most of it coming from the ship to our house."

"Still," Tom said as they took another step together, "I like to explore—you never know what you'll find. Will you come exploring with me, Tabitha?" He twisted his head and smiled down at her, that sunlit smile that made any question seem exciting.

"I'd love to," Tabitha answered, and smiled back at him. She had never heard anyone use the word *explore* when it came to New Bedford. Explore was what men did who sailed on the ships that *left* New Bedford for places like California and Hawaii and China. What was there to explore in New Bedford?

"Well, look at that," Aunt Priscilla said as they entered the warm kitchen. She looked up at Tom. "My, aren't you tall. I'd never've guessed it just seeing you in bed." Priscilla Byrd pulled a chair away from the kitchen table. "You just sit right down here," she told him, "and I'll make you a cup of that fine tea the captain brought from China."

Tom sat down and gestured at the bowl of eggs and the open sack of cornmeal that had spilled over on the table. "You're busy, Mrs. Byrd, and I'm interrupting."

"No such thing," Priscilla said as she bustled about the kitchen. "Just getting ready to make Indian pudding for Jedediah, but I've got all day. Tea first."

Indian Pudding Day. Tabitha closed her eyes, hoping that it would help her remember this moment: Tom, sitting so tall and so easy at the familiar kitchen table, her aunt smiling, and Canton wrapping his orange tabby self around Tom's booted ankles.

"Look what's here," Tom said, as he bent down and picked up Canton.

"Be careful," Tabitha warned him, "he scratches strangers—"

But the warning wasn't necessary. Canton curled up into a ball of fur on his lap and closed his eyes with bliss when Tom stroked him beneath his chin. Soon they heard a purr.

"My," Aunt Priscilla said, "I've never seen that cat cozy up like that to a stranger before. You must have a magic touch, Tom Howard."

"I'm not exactly a stranger," Tom said. "I've been in your house for close to a week now, Mrs. Byrd."

It was almost embarrassing, the way that cat took to Tom, Tabitha thought. But she felt a warm blush threaten her cheeks as she watched Tom's long, tan fingers stroke Canton's chin. Had he ever stroked a girl's face that way? she wondered. Had he ever bent back a girl's head and lowered his lips to kiss her?

Tabitha grasped the edge of the table with her fingertips and watched as Aunt Priscilla carefully measured the precious tea leaves into a blue and white teapot that her brother had also brought from China.

"A week in New Bedford usually means that you're still a stranger," Aunt Priscilla was saying to Tom. "We take a long time to accept folks around here. Generations, sometimes."

"I don't believe that," Tom said. "Look at the way you took me into your home, and you didn't even know me. New Bedford is the friendliest place I've ever been to—a lot friendlier than New York, I can tell you that."

"Get the cups, Tabitha," Aunt Priscilla said. She poured the steaming pale green tea and looked again at the young man who sat at her table as though he belonged there. "Something about you makes people feel friendly, Tom. Look at my brother—I never knew him to bring anybody else home from his crew, no matter how hurt he might have been."

"And I'll never be able to thank Captain Walker and you for taking me into your home. It's meant a lot."

"I just did what I hope someone would do for one of mine who was hurt in a strange place," Aunt Priscilla said. "Nothing more. Your mother would do the same, Tom, if you brought home a hurt shipmate."

Tom frowned and looked down into his teacup. "My mother's dead," he said quietly.

Is that why you ran away from home? The question was on the tip of Tabitha's tongue, but it never got past there. She didn't need Aunt Priscilla's warning look to stop her from asking Tom any questions. "We don't pry into other folks' doings," her aunt had told her often enough while she was growing up. "People want to confide in you, they'll do it in their own good time."

Would there ever be a time when Tom would confide in her? Would he ever share those hidden parts of himself with her? Tabitha hoped so, but she wouldn't force him to tell her anything by asking a lot of questions. Besides, the past didn't matter. Not really. Not today, when they were about to go exploring together.

Tabitha stood up. "Are you ready, Tom?"

He got to his feet, resting a hand on her shoulder for support. "I'm ready," he said, and he smiled broadly—*that* smile, the smile Tabitha could not believe he had ever smiled at anyone before.

Chapter 4

Indian Pudding Day: Ten o'clock.

Tabitha shifted her straw picnic basket to her other arm, and refused Tom's offer to carry it for her. "There's not much to see in New Bedford," she said, as they walked down the street that led to the harbor. "There are the ships, and that's the church we go to, and that's the store—"

"Can we walk away from the harbor?" Tom asked her. "I like ships but I'll be back on one pretty soon. I'd like to see something else for a change. Someplace different."

Tabitha shook her head. "There's nothing different about New Bedford, Tom. It's not like California or someplace like that. There's really no place to go exploring here."

Tom smiled, and Tabitha saw that in bright sunlight his eyes looked more green than gray. "There's always something. Let's see," Tom said, closing his eyes and pointing. "I bet that not too far from here there's a little patch of woods, and a meadow, and I bet a stream—"

"You must have second sight," Tabitha cried out. "There's a place just like that right next to Mr. Merton's farm. But how did you know?"

Tom laughed. "I didn't. Not really. I just guessed. It looks like the kind of country that might have such a place nearby."

But to Tabitha it was magic—Tom knowing where they could find the right place for their picnic.

Indian Pudding Day: Twelve noon.

"This is great," Tom said. He was stretched out beneath a willow tree that trailed its pale green branches into a cold, crystal stream. "Have you ever been here before, Tabitha?"

"Mmm, once," she said, as the sweet memory of another day and another picnic came back to her.

Tom sat up and reached for her hand. "Was it with another boy?" he asked.

"Not with a boy." Tabitha had taken off her bonnet, and her curtain of hair partially hid her face as she rummaged in the picnic basket. "It was with my mother. And I had forgotten all about it until now. But she brought me here when I was six or seven to pick violets. Look," she said, leaning over the grassy bank, "see? Violets—hundreds of them."

Tom moved so that his head was close to hers. He looked down to where Tabitha was pointing and saw the small flowers, the tiny purple blossoms twining their way between Tabitha's fingers.

He picked several flowers and inhaled the perfume. "Sweet," he said. Reaching out, he brushed the petals of the flowers against her cheek.

Tabitha felt a surge of warmth clear down to her toes. Turning swiftly, she left the violets and moved back to the picnic basket. "Lunch, Tom? Aunt Priscilla's packed enough for ten people."

"Sure," Tom said. "Being out in the air makes me hungry, a lot hungrier than staying cooped up in one room—"

"Weren't you comfortable?" she asked, wanting more than anything to hear him say that he was, to hear him say again how much he'd enjoyed her company during his convalescence.

"Course I was," Tom replied. "More comfortable than I've been since I left New York. Your whole family is wonderful, you most of all. There aren't girls like you in New York, you know."

"There aren't?" Tabitha asked too eagerly. She handed him a drumstick and added, "What's New York City like? The only big city I've ever been to was Boston."

"New York's cold and mean," Tom said, and Tabitha was dismayed to see the change that came over his face. When Tom stopped smiling she felt as though the sun had disappeared behind a cloud, and his warm green eyes looked like cold gray stone.

Tabitha nibbled on a piece of chicken and didn't say another word. She shouldn't have asked about New York City, she realized. She shouldn't have pried into Tom's past life. Now the day had changed, and it was all her fault. "I ask too many questions, Tom. Aunt Priss always says I do, and she's right. I guess I was just born curious. I'm sorry."

Tom looked up, the sun dawning as a smile curved his lips. "No, *I'm* sorry, Tabitha," he said. "There're just some things I don't like to think about. You see, after my mother died, my father married someone who didn't want me around. That's why I left home, because my father and I had a big fight about it, and that's why I hate talking about New York even though I lived there all my life, or at least until I went to sea." Tom paused. "You can't know what it was like," he continued, and Tabitha was surprised at the hurt in his voice, "but can you imagine how you'd feel if your father decided to marry someone who wanted you to leave home? So, eventually, that's what I did."

Tabitha knew that Tom didn't really expect an answer and she didn't say anything. It was a beautiful day, she thought, and they were in a beautiful place. She had never gone on a picnic with a boy before, and she didn't want to spoil the day talking about such serious things.

But what could she talk about? Tom had been to so many places, seen so many things, and she had done nothing but spend sixteen years in New Bedford. He had met girls in California, and Hawaii, and maybe even China, and they probably had lots to talk about. Tom must be bored being with dull Tabitha Walker.

Finally, she said the only thing she could think of saying, "Would you like some of Aunt Priscilla's black walnut cake, Tom? And would you like to know how to make it? It isn't really too hard once you've picked the walnuts, and once you've cracked them open. Of course that's the really hard part, cracking open the walnuts—"

Tabitha was suddenly silent again, and Tom took a bite of black walnut cake. When he looked at Tabitha she was happy to see that his eyes were a warm green once again.

"Tabitha," he said, and he dipped his fingers into the flowing stream and then shook them dry, sprinkling the violet flower faces with water, "I have to tell you—you're the prettiest girl I've ever seen in my whole life. Prettier than the girls in New York and in California, and I guess—well, prettier than anyplace where there *are* girls."

Tabitha felt her cheeks go warm with a blush. She was happy, but she didn't know what to say—she had never been alone with a boy like this before, much less a boy who told her how pretty she was. She bent forward and played with the violets again, but this time Tom moved her fall of hair behind her ear so that her face wasn't hidden from him.

"You're not mad that I said that, are you, Tabitha?"

Tabitha shook her head. "I'm not mad, Tom, I just don't know what to say. No one's ever said anything like that to me before."

He shook his head. "Everybody in New Bedford must be blind then." He stood up and held his hand out to her. "Time to go exploring."

She grasped his hand. It was warm and firm and strong. "But you've seen everything there is to see," she said.

"Maybe," Tom answered, "and maybe not."

Indian Pudding Day: Two o'clock.

Tom was right, Tabitha thought, there was a lot to see, even in a world that she thought she knew like the back of her hand. There were little ferns growing beneath oak trees, and tiny blue flowers that Tom said were the same color as her eyes.

Robins and bluejays became interesting, exotic birds, and she felt a thrill of wild, joyous freedom as they watched a flight of Canada geese fly above them in a V-formation.

A small brown and silver rabbit crossed their path, and, because they stood quietly without moving, the rabbit also stopped and remained quiet for a moment, looking up at them inquisitively.

They walked until they arrived at the stone fence that surrounded Mr. Merton's meadow, and a mare and her foal galloped up to look at the visitors. At first the chestnut horses refused to come to the fence, but Tom fished an apple from the picnic basket and held it out flat on the palm of his hand. The mare came and took the apple in one bite, her velvety lips brushing Tom's hand.

"Horses are beautiful," Tabitha said, although she had never really thought about it before, had never given a horse more than a quick glance.

"You should see them in California," Tom told her.

"Once you get inland, there are no fences there, and no houses either, just open country."

Tabitha tried to picture a land without limits. "It must be beautiful," she said. Tabitha closed her eyes for a minute, picturing herself on a horse, galloping beside Tom, the wind blowing their hair back. It was like a dream. She opened her eyes and blinked. "But," she said, suddenly dismayed, "I don't know how to ride. No one rides much in New Bedford."

Tom laughed. "I don't know how either. I mean to learn, though, someday. Then I'll teach you."

Tabitha looked up at him. His white-blond hair was blowing back from his forehead. "Are you going with the *White Swan* when she sails again?" she asked.

Tom nodded. "If your father'll have me as a hand."

Tabitha's heart beat with excitement. If her father agreed to take her with him on his next trip, she and Tom would go sailing off together, away from stuffy little New Bedford. They would see the golden coast of California and the exotic ports of China. She turned to Tom, her eyes shining. She longed to tell him of her plan to sail on the *White Swan,* but she thought better of it. First, she had to persuade her father that it was time she left New Bedford. It would be harder if he thought she had talked things over with Tom before discussing matters with him.

"Tabitha," Tom said, as if he were able to read her thoughts, "Tabitha . . ." He bent down and his lips brushed very lightly against hers. Then she was in his arms and he was kissing her.

Tabitha closed her eyes and felt her body lean into

his, as if it had a mind of its own. But suddenly she pulled back from him, realizing that she was being kissed—for the first time ever! But it wasn't Tom's first time, she was sure of that, and the idea that maybe he did this everywhere, with every girl he met, unsettled her.

"We better go back home, Tom," Tabitha said, annoyed at the slight tremor in her voice. Trying to make everything seem ordinary once again, she added, "Aunt Priss will want me to help her with dinner. We're having Indian pudding tonight."

"I know," Tom agreed, though disappointment showed in his eyes. "I guess we better start back at that." Tabitha heard a slight huskiness in his voice as he added, "Indian pudding, is it good?"

"It's wonderful," Tabitha told him, but her mind was far from Indian pudding. *How does he really feel?* she wondered. *What is he thinking? Does he really like me? Oh, I wish I had someone to talk to.*

But there was no one. Tabitha didn't have a best friend or even a mother. And Aunt Priscilla, kind as she was, would never understand. No, Tabitha would have to go by her own instincts where Tom Howard was concerned.

Chapter 5

"WELL NOW," JEDEDIAH WALKER SAID THAT NIGHT after he'd finished supper, complete with three helpings of Indian pudding, "I've been so happy to see all of you that I forgot about passing out the gewgaws I brought home."

But Tabitha knew better. That was her father's old trick. He had used it when she was a little girl. He never gave out the gifts he had brought until it was close to the time that he would be leaving again.

If Jedediah thought that his presents had ever distracted his daughter from his departure he was very much mistaken, and now that Tabitha was sixteen she knew exactly what to expect when her father gave gifts.

Tabitha knew that even as they oohed and aahed he would be clearing his throat and saying, "I think in a day or two—depending on the tides and the weather, of course—it'll be time for me to set sail again."

But this time Tabitha was ready for him. First she

admired the embroidered, dark green, silk crepe shawl that her father had brought Aunt Priscilla from China. And then she agreed that the fur-lined cape for Uncle Silas would keep him warm during the coldest weather that New England had to offer. Finally, her father slipped a wide, cream-colored jade bracelet on her wrist and Tabitha said that it was the most beautiful piece of jewelry that she had ever seen.

"Cream-colored jade is very rare," her father said, "even in China. I had to trade ten otter skins for that bracelet, Tabitha. It used to belong to a princess."

"It's beautiful, Papa," Tabitha said, but while she was turning the bracelet on her wrist, admiring the way the color of the stone changed with the different light, she was waiting. She sat up straight on the little footstool that she had placed at her father's feet, and waited. She was glad that Tom had gone to visit a shipmate right after supper—there was no need for him to hear the fuming and fussing that her family was sure to create when she told them of her plans.

"I think," Jedediah said as he tamped tobacco into the bowl of his pipe, "I think in a day or so—depending on the tides and the weather, of course—it'll be time for me to set sail again."

"So soon?" Priscilla asked, a little sadly.

Silas said nothing. He had been busy outfitting the *White Swan* for days, and he knew that Jedediah had prepared his crew.

Tabitha stopped turning the bracelet on her wrist. "To California again?"

"Yes, Daughter," Jedediah replied. "And China too."

"That doesn't give me much time," Tabitha said at last, her voice matter-of-fact to cover the beating of her heart.

"Time for what?" Jedediah asked.

"Time to get packed," Tabitha replied, her blue eyes never once leaving his face. "This time I'm going with you and the *White Swan*, Papa."

Jedediah smiled, but the smile quickly faded. "That would be wonderful, of course, Tabitha," he said, "but quite impossible."

"Tabitha," Aunt Priscilla said, "we told you that, Silas and I both. The whole idea is impossible."

"Impossible," Uncle Silas echoed.

"But why is it impossible?" Tabitha asked. "My father's a captain of a sailing ship. Why can't I sail with him?"

"Girls just *don't*," Aunt Priscilla said.

Tabitha's lips puckered in a frown, and Jedediah said, more softly than his sister, "Girls never have, Tabitha. A sailing ship has never been considered the right place for a girl."

"But Mama sailed with you," Tabitha reminded him. "What about that?"

Her father cleared his throat. "She was my wife, Tabitha. That's different."

"I'm your daughter," Tabitha persisted, her chin jutting into the air. "I can't see why it's so different."

"Because it is," Aunt Priscilla said.

Tabitha looked to her father. "Papa?" she questioned. He didn't seem to think that the idea of her sailing with him was so crazy, even if his first answer had been no. Perhaps he could be persuaded. "You could teach me to work, maybe help the cook or something. I wouldn't be in the way, I promise."

Jedediah hesitated. If it was up to him . . . but it wasn't. He glanced at his sister and saw her shocked look. Was he actually considering taking Tabitha with him? Priscilla's look decided him. She had been taking care of Tabitha for the last five years and he had to do what she thought best. Besides, what did he know about taking care of a young lady? No, he had to follow Priscilla's lead.

"I'm sorry, Daughter," he finally said as gently as he could. "Goodness knows, I'll miss you every bit as much as you'll miss me—"

"No, you won't, Papa," Tabitha said, thinking of the long, dreary New Bedford days. "You don't know what it's like, always being left behind, always *waiting—*"

If Tom Howard hadn't chosen that very moment to return, Tabitha felt that she might have been able to persuade her father to let her sail with him. But Tom did walk in, and when he heard what they were talking about he smiled at Tabitha and said, "It would be great having you along on the *White Swan!*"

That was all Captain Walker had to hear. It was this young sailor, then, that lay behind Tabitha's sudden yearning to go to sea. No, he'd not invite *that* sort of trouble on board the *White Swan*. Whether he wished to admit it or not, Tabitha was a young woman, and a beautiful one.

"You stay in New Bedford with your aunt and uncle," Jedediah Walker told Tabitha at last, avoiding the accusing glance of her blue eyes, "and there'll be no more talk about your sailing on the *White Swan*. You and Tom can say your good-byes here, in port." Tabitha's face went red with embarrassment. How could her father talk that way in front of Tom? Now Tom would think she only wanted to sail to be near *him*.

"For months now," Tabitha managed to say, looking at her father rather than at Tom, "I've been watching and waiting for the *White Swan*, because I wanted to sail with you, Papa. I told Aunt Priscilla and Uncle Silas about it long before anyone else came to this house! And now . . . now you think . . ." Tabitha couldn't finish her sentence. She stood up and ran out of the room, her cheeks fiery with anger.

"That's so, Jedediah," Aunt Priscilla said. "That's all the child's been talking about for months."

"I didn't know that," Captain Walker said. He looked around, wanting to ask Tom if Tabitha had ever discussed this preposterous sailing idea with him, but Tom had left the house.

"He's probably gone for a walk," Priscilla said. "No need for him to hear all these family matters."

"Right," Jedediah Walker grunted, getting up out of his chair. "I think I'll go for a walk, too. Need to cool off some."

He left the house, thinking that he would probably

catch up with Tom somewhere near the port, but Tom hadn't gone in that direction.

Tom circled around to the back of the house. Using the fork of an elm tree and a handy nearby trellis, he ignored his injured knee and climbed up to the widow's walk where the little heels of Tabitha's shoes tapped back and forth in the dark.

"Tabitha," he said, swinging over the railing, "Tabitha—"

She looked at him. "I suppose you think *you're* the reason I want to go to sea, just like my father does."

He stepped forward and took her in his arms. She protested at first, struggling until she saw his smile lifting above her in the moonlight. "Well, it's a mighty flattering thought, but no, I reckon you got your own reasons."

"Oh, I do, Tom," Tabitha said, her throat so full of longing that she could barely get the words out. "I can't stand staying home this way, year after year, perched up here like a crow, waiting for something to happen to me."

"Well, plenty'd happen to you on board the *White Swan,*" Tom chuckled, "but it might not all be pleasant. Even on board a sturdy ship like the *White Swan,* there are storms and danger. Your father didn't mean to hurt you, can't you see that? He's just trying to protect you. From the sea and . . ." Tom grinned and kissed her forehead, "from me too, I guess."

Tabitha could not suppress the giggle that escaped

from her lips. "Do I need protecting from you, Tom Howard?"

"Maybe," he said, "and maybe not. I think what you *mostly* need, Tabitha, is protection from yourself."

She jerked away from him. "Now you're doing it too," she protested, "treating me like a child."

Then she felt his hands on her waist, turning her toward him. "It's treating you like a woman I'm thinking of, though, Tabitha," he said. His lips grazed the soft skin along her neck. "Oh, but it would be great to sail to California with you aboard the *White Swan,*" he whispered huskily.

His kisses made flames dance along her skin. The flames grew and grew until they kindled a fire deep within her. Aunt Priscilla had taken her, once, to visit a kiln where soft, pliant clay was turned into hard pottery. The fire inside her was exactly like that kiln fire. It turned her soft, secret yearnings into firm resolutions.

"I *am* going to sail with you, Tom," she said fiercely. "I'm going to go aboard the *White Swan* and nobody is going to stop me!"

"I don't see how," Tom said. "Maybe I know Captain Walker better than you do. He's a fair man, but once he makes up his mind to something, that's it."

"You don't know Captain Walker's daughter," Tabitha said. "Once *she* makes up her mind to something, that's it, too."

Had she really said that? Tabitha could hardly believe that those words had come out of her mouth. For sixteen whole years she had never gone against her family, and now she was ready to defy them all.

Tom shook his head. He could see that Tabitha was about to break her heart over something that could never be. He walked to the railing and looked out over the roofs of the sleeping town of New Bedford. In the distance he could see the masts of the ships anchored in the port, and their gentle rocking motion in the quiet waters made him think of toy boats.

It was a beautiful sight as the full moon bathed everything with its soft light. He looked at Tabitha—her red hair looked black by night, except where the moonlight streaked it with silver.

Tom took Tabitha in his arms—it felt so natural, so right—and he gently kissed her. "Tabitha," he whispered, "promise that you'll wait for me."

"Wait for you?" Tabitha was confused and she had trouble catching her breath. "What do you mean?"

"When the *White Swan* comes back so will I," Tom said. "Four years, maybe a little less. Four years isn't such an awfully long time."

Tabitha looked up at him. The moonlight made his hair look star-white. He didn't know how long four years was, but she knew. And he didn't know about the women who paced the widow's walks of New Bedford and who waited more than four years—the women who waited forever.

"No," she whispered, "I won't wait for you, Tom. Four years is too long. . . ."

Tom let go of her, and the light of the moon showed her that he was hurt and disappointed.

They didn't speak again. Silently Tom stepped over the railing and climbed down to the ground just as he had gotten up.

It was only when she was sure that he couldn't hear her that Tabitha said, "I won't wait for you, Tom, because I'm going to be sailing on the *White Swan,* too."

Tabitha went back into her bedroom calm and determined. She could have asked for Tom's help, could have told him that nothing would stop her from sailing on the *White Swan,* but the less he knew the better it would be for him with his captain.

Her father already suspected that they were interested in each other—perhaps *too* interested—and she didn't want him to be angry with Tom during the whole long voyage.

Of course, he would be angry with her, too. But she was his daughter and he loved her. He'd forgive her, especially once he saw that she was no trouble on board ship, but he'd never forgive Tom if he thought that he had helped Tabitha behind his back. No, the less Tom knew the better it would be for him.

Tabitha smiled when she thought how pleased Tom would be once he discovered that she was on board the *White Swan.* Would her father be pleased, too? He would be, after a while. Besides, what could he do? Her father would never turn back to New Bedford once he set sail, and there would be plenty of time for forgiveness between Massachusetts and California.

Chapter 6

FOR THE NEXT FEW DAYS TABITHA WAS UNUSUALLY quiet and sweet—so quiet and sweet, in fact, that Aunt Priscilla began to look at her with suspicion. But Captain Walker urged her to leave Tabitha alone.

Saying he had to get back on board and help with the ship's preparations, Tom Howard had abruptly left the house. No doubt his absence played a part in Tabitha's dampened spirits. But let her weather the storm, Captain Walker thought. Tom was a nice lad, but the sooner she got over him the better. Sixteen was too young to be seriously involved.

"He's a nice enough young man," Priscilla said to her brother one morning over breakfast.

"He'll be even nicer in four years," Jedediah responded. "*If* he sails back here with me, he and Tabitha can talk seriously then. You don't know these young sailors like I do, Priscilla. Besides, Tabitha may not be interested in him four years from now. She's still a child, doesn't know her mind."

Priscilla Byrd looked at her brother. "Tabitha's sixteen, Jedediah. How old was her mother when the two of you got married?"

"Eighteen," he mumbled.

"Eighteen?" Priscilla echoed, her eyebrows lifting. "And how long had you been courting? About two years, wasn't it?"

"About," Jedediah admitted warily.

"Making her about sixteen?"

"Well . . . about. Besides, that was different."

Priscilla sighed. "It always is," she said, "when it's a man's daughter."

Now what was that supposed to mean? Jedediah wondered. When the proper suitor came along, he'd be glad to give Tabitha his blessing. But that, he assured himself, wouldn't be for years yet.

The morning after their meeting on the widow's walk, Tabitha wanted to tell Tom that she would be sailing on the *White Swan* with him, but she held back, determined not to let anyone know her plans. He would be so surprised, and then he would feel mean and guilty for doubting her feelings for him, she thought.

Still, it upset her terribly to know that Tom was angry with her. His words just before he had left the Byrd house made his feelings clear. "I must have been a fool to let you know how much I cared," he said. "I wasn't asking you to wait forever, Tabitha, just for four years, that's all—four short years!"

Tabitha hadn't answered him. He would understand after the *White Swan* sailed. Besides, Tom's seriousness made her feel uncomfortable. She liked Tom—liked him a whole lot. She could even say that she liked him more than any boy she had ever known, except that she hadn't known many boys all that well, and that was the problem.

Do I love Tom Howard? Tabitha wondered as she watched him go. She didn't know the answer to that question. Tom Howard had kissed her, something no boy had ever done, and that had confused everything. Maybe you felt this way about every boy that kissed you, Tabitha decided. Because kissing someone was like giving him a little piece of yourself, and once *that* was done, well, it was hard to keep a clear head about things.

Wanting to catch a full tide that week meant that Captain Walker and the *White Swan* would sail at midnight.

"We'll go down to the wharf to see you off, Jedediah," Priscilla said, sure that Tabitha would insist upon doing just that.

But to her surprise, Tabitha said, "You go ahead, Aunt Priss. I don't want to watch the *White Swan* sail away. It's hard enough waiting for her to come back. I don't want to stand on land and watch her disappear."

"You're right, Daughter," Captain Walker said, "you and I will say our good-byes here."

That evening, after their six o'clock supper, Tabitha and her father said good-bye. Jedediah felt that his daughter's hug was not as warm as he might have liked, and he thought that she was still angry with him.

"I don't like to think I'm leaving with you mad at me, Tabitha," he told her.

"I'm not mad, Papa," Tabitha said, "truly I'm not. And I hope you're not mad at me."

"Of course not," he said. "I'm going to miss you, Tabitha."

Tabitha ignored that, and said, "Let's make each other a promise, Papa."

"A promise? What kind of a promise?"

Tabitha's smile was all innocence. "A promise that if we do get angry with one another we'll never stay angry for longer than—oh, let's say . . . overnight."

Jedediah smiled, relieved to see that, for all his fears about her having grown up behind his back, she was still a child. "I promise, Tabitha," he said.

They hugged each other again, and then Tabitha said good night to her aunt and uncle who were off to see the *White Swan* sail.

"Good night, Aunt Priss," Tabitha said, giving her aunt an extra hard hug. "I love you so much."

"Land, child," Aunt Priscilla said, pleased but flustered, "I'm not going to China—just to the wharf. We'll see each other at breakfast."

Uncle Silas gave Tabitha a peck on the forehead. "That's right, see you at breakfast, Tabitha." And he, too, received an extra hug.

Tabitha waited at the door until she could no longer see them, and then she ran upstairs to her room.

She rummaged through the bottom of a wardrobe until she found a small straw suitcase that had belonged to her mother—it had been another one of her father's souvenirs from China. What should she pack? Tabitha wondered. The case was small, and she didn't want to carry anything that was too heavy or too conspicuous.

In the end, she decided to pack three dresses—two cotton and a soft, pale blue wool. She folded in her favorite white silk shawl with the large embroidered pink peonies, and then she added a wool jacket and a warm challis shawl. Shoes! Of course, another pair of shoes and her underthings, and the case was almost filled. She clasped it shut, and then opened it once again to include a night dress, a robe, and a handful of silk ribbons for her hair. It was bound to be windy on the *White Swan*, and the ribbons would hold her hair back handily.

Tabitha looked at her straw bonnet, was about to leave it, and then she thought of her Aunt Priscilla. Her aunt would be upset when she discovered that Tabitha had sailed away on the *White Swan*, but maybe she would be a little less upset if she saw that Tabitha had taken both a bonnet and a parasol—a real parasol this time, not the paper Chinese umbrella with the red-lacquered handle.

There was one more thing to do, and that was the hardest of all: she had to leave a note for her aunt and uncle to find on her pillow. But what could she say to these two people who loved her and had been so good to her?

Don't be angry, was the first thing she wrote, *I'm all right. I'm aboard the* White Swan. *I'll send a letter back to you as soon as I can. I love you, and I hope you love me still. Tabitha.*

She would have liked to thank them for everything they had done for her, but thanks were just too hard to express in a short note. When she was on board ship she would have time to write them a long letter telling them how grateful she was.

Tabitha looked for Canton, wanting to give him a good-bye pat, but Canton never thought of himself as a house cat, and he'd gone out hours before. Would he miss Tabitha? She didn't think so. Canton was too lordly to miss anyone.

Tabitha changed into a pale tan wool dress with a short jacket that buttoned at the waist. She put her new jade bracelet on her wrist and her straw bonnet on her head. The parasol and case were in her hand, and she left the Byrd house without looking back. She had waited until eleven o'clock when she knew there wouldn't be too many people on the street, and probably no one on the wharf.

If someone did see her she would say that she was bringing some things to her father on board ship, but she hoped that she would run into no one.

How would she get on board the *White Swan?* She knew that there would only be one man at watch on the gangplank, and even that man might be called away to help with the many details that had to be attended to before the ship sailed. Thank goodness her father's ship was a merchant vessel and not a naval ship—rules were not all that strict on board the *White*

Swan; she'd heard both her father and her uncle say that very thing.

Tabitha had picked her time just right. She saw no one on the streets, and those who had come to say good-bye to the crew members of the *White Swan* had long since gone home. Only her aunt and uncle were still about, and they were safely below with her father in his cabin. They wouldn't see her.

Mr. Plum, the first mate, was at the top of the gangplank when Tabitha arrived. He recognized her at once. "Decided to come say good-bye to the captain?" he asked. "And what's all that?" he said, pointing to the straw case that Tabitha was carrying.

"Papa forgot some things I had knitted for him especially; he wouldn't want to sail without them."

"Of course he wouldn't," Mr. Plum said, smiling at her. "Your father's in his cabin—you know the way."

Tabitha thanked him, adding, "Oh, and Mr. Plum?"

"Yes, Miss Walker?"

"Don't mention seeing me to my father. He gets so emotional over these farewells, I think it best to make the break as clean as possible. You understand, don't you?"

"Of course, miss," Plum replied, his round face bobbing like a cork in the torchlight. After Plum turned his back, Tabitha scooted past the stairs that led below, until she was on the far side of the ship. She saw a large, tarpaulin-covered dory and decided that it was the perfect place to hide until the ship sailed.

The tarpaulin was tied tight, but Tabitha loosened the knot, her fingers icy with nerves. She had just managed to throw her case and parasol into the dory, and then to clamber in herself, when she heard some of the crew approaching.

It was dark, and they were too busy to notice the loosened tarpaulin. Tabitha curled up quietly at the bottom of the dory, her head resting on the straw case. She felt wide awake with excitement, but she hadn't realized how tiring being a stowaway was. Even when it was still at anchor, the *White Swan* bobbed and rocked in the water. Soothed by the gentle motion, Tabitha soon fell asleep in a cramped position in the wooden boat.

Tabitha sailed away from New Bedford without being aware of it. She didn't give her birthplace one final wave, and she never watched the town disappear behind the horizon, as she had planned to do. Tabitha slept until the dipping and pitching motion of the *White Swan* made her wake with a terrible start. This was unlike the gentle rocking she had fallen asleep to, this was a violent see-sawing that flipped her stomach over and over. With a muffled cry, Tabitha realized that she was suffering from an illness that she had only heard about—she was seasick!

She tried to adjust her bonnet and straighten her dress—both impossible to do at the bottom of a dory. She moved the tarpaulin back an inch or two, and the fresh ocean breeze made her feel a little better.

Tabitha peeked out, expecting to see the night sky. But, to her amazement, the sky was streaked with pink and orange light. She saw it was dawn and it was beautiful. She had slept until morning and now, rumpled and still feeling slightly ill, she had to face her father.

She pushed the heavy tarpaulin back a bit more and, with her bonnet tied at a crazy angle, attempted to climb out of the dory. As she was doing so, she came face to face with one of the ship's crew. The man's eyes popped with astonishment when he saw the pretty young woman climbing out of the dory.

"Like some kind of red-haired mermaid she was," he told the fascinated crew members later on.

"The same mermaid was seen on board the *Lydia Galen* before plague swept the ship," a sailor warned gloomily.

"Take your gloomy thoughts overboard, Spicer," the sailor who was telling the story said. "This weren't no mermaid at all but a real flesh and blood young woman, and a beautiful one, and one what's come to bring us good luck instead of bad. For while I'm standin' there with me mouth open, she smiles as sweet as you please, and says, 'Good morning. Would you please help me out of here? I have to go and see the captain!' "

Listening to the tale, a shiver ran up Tom Howard's back, clear up to the white-blond hairs above his collar. Tabitha! It had to be. He smiled. So she had come aboard after all—done just what she wanted, in spite of her father's wishes. He'd been wrong to ask her to wait. He saw that now. A girl like Tabitha was like the tide, waiting for no one.

Chapter 7

"I CAN'T BELIEVE YOU DID SUCH A CRAZY THING," Captain Walker roared. Tabitha had never heard him speak so loudly before. "What possessed you? Your aunt and uncle must be frantic! What I should do is turn the *White Swan* about and take you back to New Bedford this instant!"

Tabitha bit her lips and said nothing. Instead, she let her father's words rain down around her, careful not to raise her eyes lest she give herself away. For the secret light of triumph lit her face. No matter what her father was saying, she knew that he would never turn the ship around to take her back home. No captain would. Once they had sailed, it was bad luck to put back again.

Tabitha knew that the worst was over now, that she was on her way. Her life had begun at last, and nothing and no one could stop it. Her father might shout, but surely—*surely*—he was a little pleased to have her on board.

When he finally took a breath, she said, "I left a

note for Aunt Priss and Uncle Silas. They know where I am, that I'm safe with you on the *White Swan*."

Captain Walker shook his head. "That was the only sensible thing you've done so far, Tabitha. But have you given a thought to what I'm to do with you? Where you're to sleep?"

"Any cabin is good enough for me, Papa," she told him. "It doesn't have to be as big as yours."

Captain Walker smiled grimly. "There isn't another cabin as big as mine, Tabitha. There isn't even another cabin available! The crew members sleep together in their quarters, and my first mate shares his cabin with the bosun. Well, I suppose you can just sleep in the dory for the rest of the trip—"

"Papa!" Tabitha cried, "you don't mean that."

"I don't," he said, "but it would serve you right if I did." And then he was off again.

But this time Tabitha reminded her father of the promise he had made in New Bedford. "If you want to stay angry with me until tomorrow morning, I guess you can, Papa—but no longer than that. Remember, you promised."

Captain Walker looked at his daughter. "And now I know why you made me make that promise, Tabitha. All right, what's done is done. I'll find you a place to sleep, and after that we'll have a little talk, young lady."

"Yes, Papa," Tabitha said quickly.

The captain had one of his men clear out a tiny cabin that held extra ship's supplies. There was a bunk there, and not much else, and Tabitha could see that her father was determined not to let her get too comfortable aboard his ship.

But it didn't matter, she thought happily, as she put the contents of her straw case on a tiny table that Mr. Plum had brought her. She had sailed away from New Bedford; she was on her way to wonderful places, and that was all that mattered—that, and the fact that somewhere on this same boat, Tom Howard was waiting to see her.

Tabitha had hoped her presence on the *White Swan* would come as a complete surprise to Tom, and she was disappointed when it didn't. Even so, the smile he gave her when he saw her almost took her breath away.

"Why didn't you tell me you were planning to stow away?" he asked in a rush. "Why didn't you let me help you?"

"Because I didn't want to get you into trouble with my father," Tabitha answered. "I want my father to like you."

Tom looked at her quizzically. There was so much he could read into a statement like that. But no, he'd already pushed her once, by asking her to wait for him. It had been a mistake; he wouldn't do the same again.

Still, Tom's heart soared, standing next to Tabitha on the deck of the *White Swan*. Perhaps this voyage would be the beginning of their life together, he thought. Perhaps with Tabitha he could find the one thing he'd always been looking for—someone to love and be with, someone to sail home to. During the long days at sea they would have time to get to know each other, time to fall in love. And he would spend every spare moment with her.

But Jedediah Walker had his own ideas about how his daughter would spend her time aboard the *White Swan*. "You'll stay up here on the bridge with me, Tabitha, as much as you can. I don't want you getting too friendly with the crew."

You don't want me getting too friendly with Tom Howard, Tabitha thought, but all she said was, "Yes, Papa."

He can't watch me every minute, Tabitha thought. *I'll see Tom.* The ship was too small for the two of them to be kept apart long. She and Tom would manage to see each other—they both knew that. And Jedediah Walker also knew it.

On her second evening at sea Tabitha strolled the deck, admiring the sunset over the water. She didn't hear the footsteps behind her, but she did feel a hand on her shoulder. She turned, expecting to see her father or Mr. Plum; instead she looked up to see Tom Howard's white-blond hair gilded by the setting sun.

"Tabitha," he said, his voice husky.

Her face lit up and she took a step toward him. Although they'd seen each other yesterday, they hadn't been alone. Not truly alone, with the sea spreading before them and only the evening breeze to keep them apart.

"Oh, Tom," Tabitha said, "I'm so happy! So happy to be here—"

He held his hands up at first, as though he wanted to ward her off. "We can't," he said, "not here. Your father—"

"Is below in his cabin, eating supper," Tabitha finished.

Tom was powerless then. He swept Tabitha into his arms, turning her eager face up to his. "Tabitha," he murmured.

She shook her flame-colored hair. "Oh, Tom, I feel so *free*—so wonderful and free. Is it always like this?"

He loosened his hold on her a fraction. *Free*. Yes, that was what mattered to her, not being with him. Tom sighed and wondered if this bright butterfly of a girl would ever be his.

"Look at that," he said, pointing to a distant pillar of fog. "Know what that is?"

Tabitha shook her head. It seemed to Tom that the smell of violets shook from her hair and clothing. "No, what?" she asked.

"Whales," Tom told her.

Tabitha's eyes lit up with wonder. "Whales? Really? Oh! I've always wanted to see what whales looked like!" And in her excitement, she clutched Tom's arm.

On the bridge, Mr. Plum watched Tabitha and Tom standing on the deck below him.

"Ah, young people," Mr. Plum observed to a lonely gull perched near him, "can't keep them apart for long. No more'n you can keep the tide from running up to the rocky shores."

Mr. Plum wasn't the only member of the crew to notice the attraction between Tom and Tabitha. The rest of the hands noticed too. And the handsome young bosun, Davy Pearson, noticed it most of all.

Chapter 8

DAVY PEARSON COULD TRACE HIS SEAFARING ANCESTORS back a hundred years and more. He liked to tell people that his forefathers had piloted the pilgrims to America, although this had never been proved.

Davy was twenty, handsome, hard-muscled, dark-haired, and as quick with his fists as he was with a joke. His ambition was as tall as the *White Swan*'s main mast: someday he meant to own and captain a boat every bit as splendid. And if he could marry a lass with a drop of the sea in her own blood, a lass who might inherit a boat herself, well, so much the better.

Tabitha Walker, with her sparkling blue eyes and tossing red hair, had caught Davy's eye from the first. Wasn't he as handsome as Tom Howard? Davy asked himself. Wasn't he as deserving of such a girl's attentions? Of course he was! And so, on their third day out to sea, Davy began his campaign to win Tabitha's heart.

"I hope you're planning on tucking that hair up into a bonnet when we reach Asia, Miss Walker," he said.

Tabitha, who had been looking out to sea, turned to

face him. Her hand floated automatically to her hair. "Hide my hair?" she questioned, taking in his smile and the dark glitter of his eyes. "Why?"

"Flame-colored hair like that?" he asked, grinning. "Why, if we run into some Turk, he's likely to offer your father five white horses for you, just to get you for his harem."

Tabitha felt her cheeks grow hot. It was improper talk—improper by New Bedford's stiff-necked standards, anyway—but it was also thrilling. It made her feel—well, valuable. "Thank you for the advice," she replied, laughing. "I'll remember to keep my bonnet on. I wouldn't want to cause my father any trouble." She shaded her eyes to see his face better. "I don't think we've met before . . ." she began.

He was beside her in an instant. "Name's Davy," he said. "Davy Pearson, bosun. Perhaps I can walk you around the deck?" And he offered his arm to her.

"Well . . ." Tabitha hesitated. She'd been waiting for Tom, hoping for a few moments alone with him. But so much time had passed and he hadn't appeared—no doubt he was being kept busy below deck. It was silly to do nothing, just because Tom wasn't around. She smiled and tipped her head. "Thank you, Davy."

Davy was nice, she thought innocently. Not as nice as Tom, of course, and not nice in the same way, but he was nice. And the way he looked at her, the way he offered her his arm and joked about Turks paying fabulous amounts of money to marry her—it made her bounce and flutter like a froth of sea foam.

Working below deck, Tom looked up at the latticed windows and saw the hem of Tabitha's skirt go by. And when he saw a pair of trousers go by with it, his heart began to knock and thump with alarm.

Dear Aunt Priscilla and Uncle Silas,

It's been many weeks since I left New Bedford, and I hope by now you've gotten over being mad at me. You certainly would give up being mad if you could see how happy I am here. Tom Howard has taught me all sorts of things about sea birds and fish and even how to tie the kinds of knots sailors tie. There's another sailor, too, who's been very nice. His name is Davy Pearson and he looks a little bit like a pirate—all black hair and eyes. I wish he and Tom were better friends.

Papa says we'll be docking at the Falkland Islands sometime soon—that's all the way down at the bottom of South America. Davy showed it to me on one of the maps.

Tom says that many of the ships that sail around Cape Horn stop at the Falklands, and I hope to give this letter to a whaling ship there which will be headed back to New Bedford.

I miss you both very much. Sometimes I even miss New Bedford (but not often!).

Your loving niece,
Tabitha Walker

Dear Sister Priscilla and Brother Silas,

I just want to reassure you that Tabitha is well

and has come to no trouble on the White Swan. *I think my girl will have her fill of sailing after this voyage.*

I believe she has learned that there is a reason why captains' daughters don't go sailing on their fathers' ships, and that's because there's nothing for them to do once they are on board. A captain's wife might find it hard going, too, but at least she has the solace of her husband's company. I'm afraid I'm not much solace or company for Tabitha.

It's a hard lesson, but I think that Tabitha will be happy in New Bedford after her experience on the White Swan.

My affectionate greetings to you both.

Your loving brother,
Jedediah Walker

Weeks later, when these two letters reached the Byrds, Priscilla and Silas could only shake their heads in wonder. "Do you suppose those two are even on the same ship?" Silas asked dryly. "Doesn't sound like it to me."

It was sunset. Red and gold shimmered on the waves between troughs of black. Tabitha's hair, burnished by long days in the sun, glowed like a lantern beside Tom—glowed so much he wanted to reach out and stroke it.

But Tabitha wasn't in a stroking mood. She was full

of chatter and bounce. "Can you climb that?" she asked, pointing at the mast and rigging that towered above them.

"Reckon," Tom replied. "I've never had the need to yet, though."

"Oh." Tabitha looked disappointed.

"Why?" Tom asked.

Tabitha shrugged. "Davy can. He told me how grand the world looks from way up there, how you can see land when it's miles and miles away, before anyone else. I bet it's wonderful."

Tom turned away. So it was Davy that was making Tabitha so restless. Darn that Davy Pearson, anyway!

Tabitha caught Tom's sudden frown. "Why don't you like Davy, Tom? He's a lot of fun."

Tom looked at her, his eyes level and gray. "Do *you* like Davy, Tabitha?"

Tabitha tossed her head, like a horse sensing a storm coming. "Course I do."

"Better than you like me?"

"Now you're being silly, Tom," Tabitha replied. *Jealous*. Tom was jealous. No boy had ever been jealous over her before and, wicked though it was, it gave her a thrill of pleasure. Besides, did liking Tom mean she was never to speak to anyone else? That *was* a silly notion, and a mistaken one. "Can't I like more than just one person?"

Tom's face showed hurt and disappointment. "But I thought . . . I thought you liked me in a special way, Tabitha."

She looked up into his eyes, too honest to hide her true feelings. "I *do* like you, Tom, better than any boy I've ever known. Davy and I are just friends."

Tom slipped his arm around her waist. "I'm not sure that's what Davy has in mind, Tabitha. Maybe you should be a little less friendly."

"Oh?" Tabitha stiffened slightly. She didn't like being told what to do. "Tell me, Tom Howard, what is it that you think Davy does have in mind?"

"Getting the *White Swan* by marrying the captain's daughter, maybe."

Tabitha twisted away from him. "What a nasty thing to say, Tom! Why, what do you know about it anyway? The idea!"

"Ssh," Tom said, trying to calm her. "Somebody'll think I'm murdering you if they hear you shouting like that. Calm down, Tabitha. I swear, you're a handful."

"Good!" said Tabitha, her voice still sharp. "If I'm such a handful, no one will want to marry me, not even Davy, so we have nothing to argue about."

"I don't know about that," Tom said. "I might."

"Might what?"

"Might want to marry you."

"Oh!" Tabitha gasped. She felt a bolt of lightning surge through her. Tom had asked her once before to wait for him, but that had seemed so vague and distant. Now the words *marry you* sprang to life before her. She felt Tom's arm slide around her again, pulling her to him. Beneath his clothes she felt the firm, insistent strength of his body. His lips grazed her temples.

"What do you say, Tabitha?" Tom asked.

She bit her lip. Confusion filled her with a queasiness that made seasickness seem like a mere tickle of the stomach. She liked Tom, yes, maybe even loved him—but marriage and all the things that went with it? Finally, she asked the only question that made any sense to her. "What would I do, if I . . . ," she paused, blushing, "if we were married, Tom?"

His eyes brightened. "Oh, Tabitha, I'd get you the nicest little house, and every time I came home from a sail we'd have the best time, go adventuring and exploring, like we did that day in New Bedford."

Indian Pudding Day, she remembered. But what came between pudding days? "Could I go sailing with you, Tom?"

He laughed and kissed her. "Oh, no, Tabitha. You're too precious to risk at sea. And then, soon we'd have children and you *couldn't* leave them."

Tabitha pulled away from him, frowning. "That's what I thought," she said.

"Well, it's no mystery," Tom said. "It's in the nature of things."

"But *I'm* not in the nature of things, Tom," she replied passionately. "I'm not ready to stay home yet—why, my life has just started, don't you see?" Tom let go of her. "So I'm going to have to say no, Tom. I'm not ready to marry yet." She started to walk away from him, her skirt swaying pertly. She turned and smiled over her shoulder at him. "But don't worry—I'm not going to marry Davy Pearson, either."

Now what did that mean? Tom wondered. Did it

mean that she wouldn't marry him ever or that she would marry him sometime? Lord, but she was the most beautiful, confusing girl he'd ever met. He'd just asked her to marry him, but he was no closer to knowing her mind now than he'd been an hour ago.

Chapter 9

TOM AND DAVY BOTH HAD BEEN BUSY ALL DAY, AND Tabitha was becoming bored. Not *very* bored, she told herself—not bored enough to mention it to her father, and certainly not bored enough to go to her cabin and read, as he had suggested she do.

"Another nice day," Mr. Plum said, beaming at her.

It was the same greeting he offered every morning, and this morning Tabitha responded, "I wish it were a little less nice. A storm might be an interesting change."

The first mate's smile disappeared. "You don't know what you're saying, Miss Tabitha. No sailor wants a storm at sea. You wouldn't want one either, if you'd ever been in one."

Tabitha didn't say anything, but she *did* want a storm at sea—at least a little one. The idea of pouring rain and wild, gusty winds excited her.

They were about two days away from the Falkland Islands when Tabitha got her wish.

It looked like an ordinary morning. The sky was clear and the sea was calm. If anything, the sea was calmer than Tabitha had ever seen it, and the rising sun was a brighter orange than usual—it had an extra glow surrounding it, like a halo.

Tabitha was first with her greeting that morning for Mr. Plum. "Beautiful morning," she said, smiling.

He looked at her glumly. "Were you wishing for a storm, Miss Tabitha?" he asked.

She laughed. "Well, as a matter of fact—"

"As a matter of fact, you're about to get your wish." He looked up at the sky. "There's a big storm heading our way," he said bleakly, "and it's coming fast."

Tabitha looked at the water and sky. "But it looks so calm."

"Calm before the storm," Mr. Plum said, "maybe you know that saying?"

"No need to go scaring my daughter, Plum," the captain said, coming up to the ship's railing.

But Tabitha's blood was pumping through her veins and her eyes glittered as they searched the horizon. "I'm not scared, Papa," she protested.

The captain and Mr. Plum exchanged glances. "Nevertheless, when the storm comes, Tabitha, I want you below in my cabin," her father said. "You'll only be in the way on deck."

"But Papa—"

"I want you below," Jedediah Walker repeated, and he gave rapid orders to Plum, who called Davy Pearson to his side.

For once, Davy seemed not to notice Tabitha's presence. He sprang into action as if fire burned beneath his feet, calling to the crew in a loud, commanding voice. Tabitha had never seen men move as quickly as the crew of the *White Swan* did then. Some sails were shortened, others were furled. Hatches were tightly shut, coils of rope and anything else that wasn't nailed down were placed below deck, and the dories were secured even more tightly.

Looking at the calm, tranquil sky, Tabitha didn't believe that anything was going to happen. It would be delightful if it did, of course. But how could it storm when the sea was smooth as a baby's cheek?

But the storm did come, whirling down upon them so quickly that Tabitha barely had time to catch her breath.

The sky, the water, and the temperature all changed in minutes. The bright orange sun disappeared into a leaden, dark gray sky, rain descended in thunderous sheets, and the calm sea came to a boil. The ship pitched forward and then back as it was caught in the trough of one wave after another, and Tabitha's stomach gave an uneasy lurch.

"Get below!" Jedediah Walker shouted as he ran past her. "Hurry!"

Tabitha tried to get to her cabin—she really *tried*. But she was too caught up in the excitement of the moment to do what she was supposed to do. She started down the steps, but she didn't move past the partial shelter she had gained by moving below deck two steps.

She had to *see*. It was frightening, but it was glorious, too! The most exciting thing she had ever seen. And then in a flash of lightning she saw the figure of a sailor climb up into the rigging; he was trying to secure a loosely flapping sail.

It was early morning, but the sky was so dark it seemed as though they had entered another night. Dark as it was, another flash of lightning showed her that the man moving up the rigging had hair as fine and light as spun gold. *Tom!* Her heart raced, remembering Tom's admission that he had never before been challenged to make the long dangerous climb into the rigging.

Tabitha climbed up the two steps and was on deck once again. The wind ripped off her shawl and pushed her back against a swinging dory. She clutched at the doorway that led below deck and tried moving forward again. She looked up and saw Tom holding onto the rigging. And then she saw Tom lose his footing.

Tabitha screamed, but no one heard her above the noise of the storm. Her blood froze in her veins. Cold water coursed down her. Then she saw Tom regain his footing. He was trying to make his way down the rigging by moving hand over hand. He had almost made it, when another blast of wind tore the rigging from his hand and he fell to the deck.

Tabitha could see that Tom wasn't moving and she tried to get to him, but the wind held her in its grip. Then, suddenly, the wind reversed, and with it at her back she was blown toward Tom.

"Tom," she shouted, bending over his unconscious

body, "Tom!" She cradled his head on her lap and rubbed his cheeks with her hands. *"Tom!"*

His eyes fluttered open and he smiled. There it was, right in the middle of this storm, the sunlit smile she remembered from New Bedford. "I guess I climbed that rigging for you, Tabitha," he murmured. "Tried, anyway."

It was then that Tabitha heard a frightening sound—a *c-r-a-c-k* that seemed louder than thunder. She looked up and saw what had made that terrifying noise. One of the masts had been hit by lightning, and the top half was bent and swayed drunkenly above them.

It's going to fall, Tabitha thought, *and it's going to fall on us.*

She wouldn't leave Tom's side, and she could see there wasn't time to call for help. She knew what she had to do. Taking Tom by the shoulders, she dragged and pulled him across the deck. She didn't have the strength to move him far, but she managed to move him a foot or two.

Tabitha heard that awful cracking noise again and she bent over Tom, shielding his body with her own. She shut her eyes tight, then she felt a rush of wind blow across her face, and heard a loud crash.

It was only a few seconds later and her father's arms were around her. "You're all right, Tabitha—thank God you're all right."

She opened her eyes, and saw the broken mast on the deck—it had fallen only inches away from them.

Captain Walker managed to get Tabitha to her feet and crew members came to carry Tom below.

"Tabitha," the captain said to his shivering daughter, once they were safe in his cabin, "you could have been killed."

"I know, Papa," she said, "I know. But we weren't." Her voice trembled, not with fear but with the wonder of what she'd done—raced to save Tom's life without a thought for her own. Would she have done the same for Davy Pearson? she wondered. Or was it Tom—only Tom—who had such power over her?

The idea that anyone at all had power over her was strange. Hadn't she protested and rebelled her whole life long? Hadn't she come to sea to taste the wild, intoxicating wine of freedom?

Yes, yes, yes, Tabitha told herself, that was all true. Then shouldn't the very thought of Tom's power over her fill her with angry dislike? Certainly it should. But it didn't. Instead it filled her with a deep, almost sleepy, happiness. She thought again and again of the moment when Tom's head had lain cradled in her lap, when she'd felt that the two of them were really one person. The deliciousness of that thought wouldn't completely leave her. For the first time in her life, Tabitha wasn't certain that freedom was all she'd thought it to be.

The *White Swan* limped toward the Falklands for repair. In her own narrow cabin, Tabitha tossed and turned and dreamed of a wind so strong it tore the words *I love you* from her lips and turned them into white birds that circled in the air above her head.

In the sailors' cabin below the mast, Tom Howard swung happily in his hammock, staring at the beams above his head and thinking joyously, *She does care for me! She must care—maybe more than she knows. She wouldn't have risked her life if she didn't love me!*

Chapter 10

TABITHA STOOD AT THE RAIL OF THE *WHITE SWAN*, straining for her first glimpse of the Falkland Islands. At first, they looked like nothing more than gray rocks on the horizon. But as they sailed closer, she saw the gray turn to green, then she saw trees and a few houses, too. The ship rounded into a channel, and Tabitha saw other ships lying at anchor. Ships and land. They had arrived at the Falklands at last!

"Papa," she asked the captain, "how soon before we can go ashore?"

"We'll anchor, Daughter, and some of us'll go ashore in the dory."

Tabitha's eyes were bright with excitement. "I can come too, can't I?"

"Well," Captain Walker hesitated, "yes, you can come—*if* you promise to stay out of trouble."

"Me?" Tabitha asked with exaggerated innocence. "What kind of trouble could I possibly get into?"

"I don't know," Captain Walker replied, "and I don't want to find out. Understood?"

Tabitha nodded, but her eyes were busily scanning the bustling port.

The dory pulled away from the *White Swan* and had to anchor a few yards off the rocky shore. Tabitha looked down at her black kid shoes with dismay. She wasn't really dressed for wading.

"It's all right, Tabitha," Davy Pearson said, and he picked her up easily in his arms and carried her ashore.

Tom Howard, one of the sailors assigned to row the dory, scowled darkly. Tabitha could see his eyes staring at her over the top of Davy's shoulder.

"Maybe you'd best put me down, Davy," she said as soon as his feet were firmly on the pebbly sand. But he held her an instant longer than necessary.

"Sure you wouldn't like me to carry you on a tour of the island? Save your feet."

Tabitha laughed. Tom, still scowling, was wading toward them with the other men.

"My feet will be fine," Tabitha said, struggling in his arms. "Besides, I think you're to go with my father and Mr. Plum to see about having repairs made."

Davy sighed. "The miseries of rank," he said, setting her gently on the sand. Tabitha swayed a little. "It feels funny," she said, as Davy steadied her. "I'm standing on land and it doesn't feel *solid*."

"You'll get used to it in a few minutes," Tom said, coming up to give her a steadying hand. "Land legs and sea legs, they both take a little time." He turned to Davy. "Captain Walker wants you," he said coolly.

Tabitha turned and waved at her father, who was

standing a short distance away. "Can Tom show me around, Papa?" she asked.

Captain Walker nodded. "But don't go far and don't get into trouble. Tom, I'm holding you responsible."

"Aye, aye, sir," Tom called back.

Now it was Davy Pearson's turn to scowl, as Tabitha and Tom walked off together. He was left with Captain Walker and the other men. There was much to do: the mast had to be repaired, food stocks replenished, and water kegs filled. With all his heart, Davy envied Tom Howard.

Tabitha and Tom walked along the beach slowly at first, but once Tabitha became more comfortable on land, she felt like running. It was wonderful having all that space before her, instead of the small, confining deck of a ship.

"Come on, Tom," Tabitha said, "let's go exploring," and she began to sprint down the beach.

Tom ran behind her, admiring the way her red hair flew behind her like a banner. She had changed some since New Bedford, he could see that. Before, she had dreamed of adventure, waited for it to come calling on her. Now she went after it with arms wide open and hair flying in the wind. But would she ever have her fill of adventuring? he wondered. Would she ever slow down enough to find that loving each other was all the adventure either of them would ever need? That was a question he didn't know the answer to.

Tabitha hadn't realized just how far she had run, but suddenly she was out of breath, and had a stitch in her side. She turned and looked back—Tom was right behind her, but she could no longer see the *White Swan*. Tabitha took a few steps up the beach, and then sat down on a sand dune, careful to avoid the tall, spiky grass that grew all around.

"I can't move another step," she gasped, "but it was wonderful."

Tom looked at her flushed face and sparkling eyes. "*You're* wonderful," he said.

Tabitha turned her head away slightly. She didn't want that kind of conversation just now. Maybe if she had stayed in New Bedford she would have been happy to hear it, but New Bedford was not the same as the Falkland Islands. Now that they had arrived at their first destination, Tabitha saw that there was so much more for her to see—California, China, the whole world! Time to talk about deep feelings later on. Right now she just wanted to enjoy the world around her.

"Tom," Tabitha said, standing up and looking about, "what's that?" She pointed to something moving in the shadow of a rock.

"It's a seal," Tom said, "a baby seal. Its mother must have been killed by a hunter—seals never abandon their babies."

"That poor thing," Tabitha said, and started running toward the little animal.

"Hold on." Tom pulled her back. "Move slowly, Tabitha, it'll try to get away if you scare it—come up on it slow."

Tabitha followed Tom, and as they came closer, Tabitha could see that the baby seal's fur was a puff of white. It raised its head, and its large dark eyes looked up at them questioningly.

"It's darling," Tabitha said.

"Ssh." Tom moved to the right, standing between the seal and the water. "Now, go up to it—but go slow."

Tabitha took one small step at a time. The baby seal squealed and tried to flop away, but Tom stood between it and possible escape into the water. The seal used its flippers to flop back and away. Tabitha sat down a little distance away. The seal whimpered as Tabitha stretched out one hand, and it shivered until it felt Tabitha's hand petting its furry head ever so gently. The baby seal squeezed its eyes shut, and its soft body flopped down contentedly at Tabitha's knees.

"It's like Canton," Tabitha said with delight, "only *so* much sweeter."

Tom sat down beside the girl and the baby seal. As he watched, the seal lifted its head and looked at them quizzically. Then it inched forward until its head rested on Tabitha's knee.

"Tom, it's adorable. What's going to happen to it without a mother?"

Tom shrugged. "I don't know."

"I bet you do, too," Tabitha said. "Tell me."

"Well, I think it may be too young to catch fish for itself. A hunter might get it—or . . . well . . . maybe it'll just starve."

"No!" Tabitha moved so abruptly that the seal sat

up, frightened once again. "We can't let that happen, Tom. We'll take it back to the ship."

"A seal? On board ship? Your father'd have a fit, Tabitha. He'd hang me from the yardarm for letting you do it. Look, Tabitha, exploring's one thing—turning the *White Swan* into a zoo is another."

But Tabitha wasn't moved. "Papa doesn't have to know," she said casually, stroking the seal's head, "not until after we've sailed."

"Tabitha—"

"He won't be able to do anything after that. I mean, he wouldn't throw it overboard, would he? He didn't throw *me* overboard, after all."

"Not yet," Tom muttered.

"Well, I don't care," Tabitha said. "I won't leave it. Look at it, Tom. Could you leave it behind to die?"

The seal raised its head and looked up at Tom.

"I guess not," Tom said. "I just hope the captain doesn't get any ideas about putting me in irons, or anything like that."

"Well, he'll just have to put the both of us in irons, then," Tabitha said.

Tom tried another approach, one that probably wouldn't work with Tabitha—logic. "How are we going to get the seal on board? I suppose you've got that figured out, too."

"Hmm," Tabitha thought. "Well, you'll have to lend me your jacket."

"Wait a second," Tom protested. "I spent all last

night polishing the buttons on this jacket, and you're going to wrap some *seal* in it?"

Tabitha's large blue eyes blinked at him. So did the seal's large black eyes. "Well," she said, "if that's how you feel . . ."

"It is."

"Then I'll just have to go find Davy Pearson. *He'll* help me."

"Now wait a minute," Tom said, and Tabitha could see that he was already peeling off his jacket. "I didn't say I *wouldn't* do it, did I?"

Tabitha smiled. Who would ever have imagined you could get men to do things so easily? Quickly, she explained her plan to him.

Tom couldn't believe that Tabitha's scheme would work, but it did. The seal was small enough for Tabitha to hold in her arms beneath her shawl. The animal's furry head peeped out from the folds, but that was hidden when Tom draped his blue jacket over Tabitha's shoulders.

"The dory makes more than one trip to the *White Swan*, doesn't it?" Tabitha asked. "Carrying supplies and all, it's bound to."

"Yes," Tom said, picturing Captain Walker's face when he discovered a seal aboard his ship.

"We'll have to go back to the *White Swan* right away. That way, we can get him hidden before Papa gets back aboard the ship."

"*We?*" Tom echoed. "I only volunteered to lend you my jacket. Where does all this *we* business come in?"

Tabitha looked disappointed. "Well, I'd hate to think you're *that* afraid of my father, Tom."

"I didn't say I was *afraid* of him, Tabitha."

"Good," she replied jauntily. "Then you will help me hide him." Tom sighed, but Tabitha went right on talking. "Now all we have to do is get down the beach and into that boat. If anyone else in the dory sees the seal, they won't say anything, will they?"

"I sure hope not," Tom said, rolling his eyes at the clear blue sky.

Tabitha and Tom walked slowly up the beach, to where the dory was bobbing in the water. Tabitha's father was nowhere in sight but the little boat, laden with supplies, was just about to leave. "Tell my father I've gone back to the ship," Tabitha told an oarsman as Tom prepared to lift her and carry her to the boat.

Davy Pearson, who was already in the boat, noticed Tom's jacket draped over Tabitha's shoulders. "Want my jacket, too, Tabitha?" he asked with a grin. "You're welcome to it."

Tabitha smiled, cradling the seal in her arms as Tom lifted her. "No thanks, I'm warm enough. I hope you're not too cold," she said to Tom.

"I'm fine," Tom gasped, "for now."

"Having trouble?" Davy asked, seeing Tom struggle. "I'd be more than happy to carry her for you."

"No thanks," Tom said, his mouth tightening into a grim line. "I'm doing just fine!"

Tabitha wanted to laugh. Only she knew what trouble Tom was having, with the frightened young seal thrashing about beneath her shawl. Then, suddenly, with one swift wriggle, the seal shot out of her arms and into the water.

"My seal!" Tabitha cried in despair. "Tom—don't let it get away!"

Tom set Tabitha back on her feet—right smack in the water—and lunged for the seal. Tabitha went splashing after him, her shoes and dress growing soggy with sea water. "My seal!" she cried again. "Oh, please, don't let him get away—he'll starve!"

The stunned sailors were staring at the spectacle in shock—the flapping, splashing seal, young Tom Howard floundering after it, and the captain's drenched daughter.

Why doesn't somebody do something? Tabitha wondered anxiously. Then she remembered something she had only recently discovered: there was one sure way to get men to do things for you. "I'll give any man who catches it a kiss!" she cried, and smiled as she saw the results of her offer. Suddenly, Tom had help in the chase, though he took time to send a scowl back her way.

Davy Pearson threw himself face down in the water, right on top of the baby seal, who managed to paddle free.

"Harder to catch then a greased pig," another sailor said, and he went into the water, too.

"I've got him," Tom said at last, his clothes sopping wet, and a note of triumph in his voice. "I've got him."

They all clambered into the dory. Everyone was

wet, including Tabitha, but the seal was in her arms again, and he seemed content enough for the moment.

"This is never going to work, you know," Tom muttered, sitting beside her. But Tabitha ignored him and listened instead to the men as they laughed and joked about what had just happened.

"You won't tell my father, will you?" Tabitha asked, pushing her damp hair behind her ears. She looked as bewitching as a mermaid.

"Not a one of us," Davy Pearson said stoutly. And he turned to look at the others. "The man who speaks first to Captain Walker will have me to fight it out with."

But Davy's threats weren't needed. Sailing could be a boring life for those who did it year in and year out, and Tabitha and her seal offered as much adventure as they had known in months.

"Your secret's safe," another sailor assured her, and the rest nodded their agreement.

"Now we got us two mascots," one of them said.

"Mascots?" Tabitha asked.

"Well," he said with a broad smile, "the way you saved Tom's life during the storm, we figured *you* to be our good luck charm, Miss Tabitha—sort of a mascot. And now your seal is the second one."

Tabitha got on board the *White Swan*, ran down to her cabin, deposited the seal on the floor, and quickly changed into dry clothes.

"I'll find you something to eat before my father

comes back," Tabitha said to the seal, who tried to follow her out of the cabin. "You stay here and be good."

Tabitha hurried to the galley. She had told the seal to be good, but just what did a good seal do? And how about a bad seal?

"Chang," she said to the ship's Chinese cook, "I'm feeling a little hungry. Could I have something to eat? Fish would be nice."

Chang looked at her blandly and handed her a tin pannikan filled with milk and a dish of what looked like crushed sardines.

"Will that do, Miss Tabitha?" he asked. "Davy had the milk sent in from the island. It will be good for a day or two."

He knew. It hadn't taken long for all the men to know that Tabitha had brought a baby seal on board—she just hoped that her father wouldn't find out as quickly.

Tabitha raced back to her cabin. The seal was all atremble in his strange new situation, but Tabitha managed to calm him with the milk, which he sniffed first, and then slurped up in eager gulps.

She was trying to interest him in the sardines when there was a knock on her cabin door. Tabitha looked around frantically—where could she possibly hide a seal?

"It's me, Tabitha," Tom Howard whispered. "Open the door."

Tabitha opened the door and stood looking at Tom. His clothes were still damp and his white-gold hair hung down over his eyes. He stepped into her cabin and closed the door behind him.

"I know what you've come for," Tabitha said.

Tom looked startled. "You do?"

She glanced up at him. "To collect your kiss, of course. After all, you *were* the one who caught my seal."

Tom began to grin, and his grin widened into a laugh. "I forgot all about that. Well, I think I'll wait, Tabitha, and have you owe me that kiss for a while longer."

Tabitha felt an unaccountable surge of disappointment. "Why did you come, then?" she asked with a toss of her head.

Tom opened the door and reached out into the hallway for the large wire cage he'd left there. "To bring this," he said. "When we left New Bedford, Chang had some live chickens in here. If we put your seal in it, we can bring him up on deck."

"But Papa will see him."

"Not if we put him in front of the fo'c's'le—you can't see that corner from the bridge."

"But the other men will see him."

"The other men already know," Tom said. "Come on, Miss Good Luck Charm, and bring your mascot with you."

With a little bit of coaxing, Tabitha and Tom got the seal into the wire cage, and carried it up on deck. They placed it right next to the forecastle of the *White Swan*.

"Will he be all right here?" Tabitha asked.

"He'll be fine," Tom said. He looked at her quizzically.

"Is something wrong, Tom?"

"Wrong? No. I was just debating whether to take that kiss now or not." And he reached for her but, laughing, Tabitha turned and slipped away. That was all right, Tom thought. He would wait.

Chapter 11

TABITHA AND THE CREW OF THE *WHITE SWAN* KNEW there was no way that the seal could be kept from Captain Walker all the way from the Falklands to California; they just hoped that the animal wouldn't be discovered until they were safely beyond the Falklands. They didn't want the captain to take the seal—which Tabitha had named Snowball—and return him to the beach.

Snowball was remarkably cooperative for a few days. He drank the milk provided by Chang, was beginning to take an interest in raw fish, and flopped about on deck following Tabitha whenever she let him out of his cage.

They had left the Falklands behind when Snowball discovered that he had a voice. He had been making soft whimpering sounds, but one morning when Tabitha was having breakfast with her father, they both heard a loud bark.

Tabitha bent her head over her plate and did her best to pretend she had heard nothing. But then there it was again!

The captain pushed his plate back. "What in tarnation—?"

Tabitha looked up just as Snowball barked again. "What?" she asked, trying to look innocent.

"Tabitha," Jedediah Walker roared, "have you brought a dog aboard the *White Swan?*"

"No, Papa," Tabitha said, happy that she could answer truthfully, "absolutely not."

"There it is again." Captain Walker stood up. Another loud bark caused a look of realization to sweep over his face. "By the stars, I know a seal when I hear one."

"A seal?" Tabitha echoed. "Oh, Papa, that's ridiculous. Maybe one of the men has a bad cough."

"No one in my crew makes such a racket," the captain said, and he hurried out of the cabin.

"Papa," Tabitha called, trailing after him, "I think I better tell you—"

But it was too late to tell him anything. Captain Walker was hurrying toward the barking sound, and when he rounded the forecastle he came face to face with Snowball, who had grown considerably since coming on board. As for Snowball, he looked up at Captain Walker with more indignation than fear. Then, seeing Tabitha behind him, he barked a cheerful hello.

"Tabitha," the captain roared, turning around and almost bumping into his daughter. "Tabitha—"

"I'm right here, Papa," she said, "no need to shout so."

"Tabitha—"

"He's no trouble, Papa, honestly," Tabitha explained quickly. "I've had him since the Falklands, and you didn't even know he was here, did you? Oh, Papa, he was all alone on the beach with no mother and he would have starved to death—or a hunter would have killed him—" Tabitha ran out of breath.

Captain Walker looked at her sternly. "Did Tom Howard know about this? I told him to keep you out of trouble."

"It was my idea, Papa," Tabitha said truthfully. "Tom tried to talk me out of it—really he did—but you know how I can be."

"Yes, yes," said Captain Walker. "I know how you can be, Tabitha." He looked heavenward. "A seal on board the *White Swan*. I suppose it'll be live horses next."

By now a crowd had gathered around them. "A seal isn't so strange as all that, Captain," Mr. Plum volunteered, stepping forward, "I once heard of a whaling ship that kept a seal as a mascot—"

"And birds," Davy Pearson chimed in, winking boldly at Tabitha. "I've heard of ships with pet canaries, and birds like them . . . them . . . parakeets, too."

"Many ships have parrots," another sailor added.

"And do you know that old whaler out of Gloucester? *Jupiter* was its name—they had a goat."

The captain looked at everyone around him, then he spied Tom Howard's halo of sun-bleached hair. "I haven't forgotten your part in this, Tom Howard," he said sternly.

Tabitha came swiftly to Tom's defense. "Don't hold it against Tom, Papa. I told you, bringing Snowball aboard was my idea. Besides, it's done now so there's no use going on about it."

Captain Walker drew in a deep breath. "That seal," he said, "is to be kept in his cage—I don't want him wandering all over the ship, is that understood? And as for taking care of him—"

"I'll help Tabitha, sir," Tom Howard said quickly.

"And me—" said Davy Pearson, glaring at Tom.

"And me—" Mr. Plum offered.

"All right, all right," the captain shouted, "just make sure that the blasted animal doesn't get under my feet. And if we see a colony of seals off the coast he can go join his fellows."

"Only if they look friendly, Papa," Tabitha said.

"Ah," the Captain said, shaking his head and hurrying toward his cabin, "seals! What next? *Friendly* seals!"

Snowball was growing. Quickly. In the two weeks since her father had learned of his presence, he had outgrown his wire cage. He could climb stairs and rove back and forth across the decks.

"That seal'll be steering this boat himself soon," Captain Walker muttered. "Time to be on the lookout for a seal colony, Tabitha."

Tabitha knew her father was right. Looking at Snowball, she could hardly believe he had once been small enough to tuck under her shawl. He had grown far too large to pick up, and the gray-black of his adult coat was quickly replacing his white baby fur.

And his barks—his barks were loud enough and mournful enough to wake the dead.

"What do you suppose is wrong with him, Mr. Plum?" Tabitha asked the first mate early one morning. It was barely dawn, and Snowball's barks were especially piercing.

"We're coming close to land," Mr. Plum replied. "Like as not he smells it. And then too, a seal that size is wanting the water. In the nature of things, he should be swimming on his own by now."

Tabitha ran her hand over Snowball's head, but she could no longer comfort him as she once had. She could see that Plum was right—Snowball yearned for the water. She turned to the first mate.

"Is anyone else up yet, Mr. Plum?"

"Just the dawn watch," he replied.

"Not my father?"

"No, miss. You know it's not your father's custom to be on deck for another hour or more."

"Good," Tabitha answered, smiling broadly. "Come on, Snowball," she said coaxingly. Then she turned back to the first mate. "Snowball and I are going to get in the dory," she said, "and when we do, would you be so good as to have us lowered over the side?"

Mr. Plum's eyebrows shot up. "What, miss?"

"Over the side, Mr. Plum," Tabitha called over her shoulder as she climbed into the dory. "Snowball is going to have his swim."

Well, thought Plum, summoning one of the dawn

watch to help him, there couldn't be much harm in that. They were in shallow waters, and the wind had all but becalmed them. Snowball could have his swim and be back topside before Captain Walker appeared on deck for the day.

But once lowered to the water, a strange desire seized Tabitha. As she watched Snowball's sleek shape glide through the water, she yearned to join him. She knew how to swim, of course—all New Bedford girls did. But she had never gone swimming in the middle of an ocean. And certainly she had never gone swimming with a seal.

As if able to read her thoughts, Snowball raised his head and looked at her inquisitively. His large, dark eyes were shiny and his whiskers quivered with pleasure. It was all the coaxing Tabitha needed.

"Oh, all right, Snowball," she said, and in a minute she was standing up in the little dory. Plum watched in shock as she stripped off her dress and petticoats and, wearing only her chemise and pantalets, plunged into the water.

It's wonderful. That was Tabitha's first thought as she felt the sea grab her hair and fan it all around her. She took a few strokes, enjoying the feeling of the warm, caressing water as it surrounded her.

Then, suddenly, Snowball surfaced beside her. She put out her hand and he slid away from her, only to circle back again and look at her with searching eyes. Then Tabitha had an idea. She grasped his tail.

Snowball shot off, paddling with his strong flippers and towing Tabitha behind him. He did not dive too deeply or stay below the surface too long. *It's almost as if he understands I need air,* Tabitha thought with delight.

She didn't know how long they'd been playing this game when she became aware of Mr. Plum shouting from the railing. "Miss Tabitha!" he was crying in alarm, his round face purple with fright. "You must come up at once! Your father will never forgive me!"

Tabitha laughed up at him. "Don't worry, Mr. Plum," she called. "I'm a very good swimmer. So is Snowball." And she caught the seal's tail as he glided by again.

Tabitha didn't hear the splash at the side of the boat—she was underwater at the time—but she *did* feel something grasp firmly at her foot.

"What? *Oh!*" she sputtered, letting go of Snowball's tail and breaking the surface of the water. Whatever it was, was still grabbing her foot, and suddenly her mind was filled with all the stories of tortoises, giant clams, and man-eating sharks the sailors had told her. "Help!" she cried. "Help!"

But then a drift of white-gold hair surfaced beside her, and two eyes exactly the same green color as the sea.

"Help, did you say?" Tom Howard laughed. "Did I hear the very independent Miss Tabitha Walker call for help?" Deftly, he encircled her waist with one arm and pulled her to him.

"Let go of me!" Tabitha cried, her legs threshing against his in the water. Tom had no shirt on—only his sailor's pants—and his firm, strong muscles rippled beneath his sun-browned skin. Tabitha planted her hands firmly against his bare chest and pushed. "How dare you scare me like that? Why, you could have drowned me—drowned us both! Now let *go* of me."

Tom grinned at her. "Sorry," he said jauntily, "but I'm under orders. Mr. Plum told me I was to jump overboard and rescue you."

Tabitha continued to struggle, but her strength was no match for Tom's. Soon he had her in the dory that floated alongside the *White Swan*. With a bit more coaxing, he was able to get Snowball into the little boat as well.

"It's all right now, Mr. Plum," he shouted up at the first mate. "You can start raising us up."

Just as the pulleys began to turn, Snowball sat up and gave the loudest, deepest bark Tabitha had ever heard. From an island that lay like a cloud in the distance came an answering bark. Snowball barked again and Tabitha, suddenly fearful, twined her arms around the seal's neck.

But the answering bark came again and Snowball broke free of her embrace. In one swift, powerful movement he flopped over the side of the dory and into the water.

"Snowball!" Tabitha cried, jumping to her feet. "Oh, Tom, help me get him back!"

Tom grabbed her hand to steady her. "Let him go, Tabitha," he said softly. "Let him go. It's time, now, and he wants to be with his mates."

Tabitha sat back down. Once the dory was safely on deck, she picked up her clothes and walked silently to the place in the forecastle where Snowball's cage had been. She felt drained. Drained and empty. And there was another feeling too, a strange one. It was a feeling of envy—envy of Snowball, who was off to live and mate and find a home with others of his kind. Suddenly, Tabitha felt rootless, splashed this way and that in the world with nothing and no one to hold her. Why had such a life ever seemed appealing to her, she wondered?

"Tabitha?" She shivered as she felt Tom's hand on her bare shoulder. "Tabitha?"

She turned to him, to his arms, and it was like turning to sunlight itself. His tawny chest pressed against her and his arms folded around her. In that one swift second, she found the home that had been waiting for her all along.

"Tom," she said, tipping her head back and looking up into his eyes. There was so much she wanted to tell him, so much she wanted to explain. But her thoughts were as tangled as seaweed. "Oh, Tom," she gasped, and turned her eager lips up to his.

That was how Captain Walker found them—nearly naked and locked in each other's arms. *"Tabitha!"* he roared. "Tabitha, go to my cabin at once! Tom Howard, I could have you whipped for this!"

Tabitha whirled on her father. "Tom didn't do anything, Papa!" she cried, and the defiance in her eyes startled her father—it was a woman's defiance, not a girl's. "You can't whip him for something that was both our faults!"

"Go to my cabin, Tabitha!" Captain Walker thundered again. "And wait there. Tom, I'll deal with you later."

The upshot was that Tabitha was to be put off the boat as soon as possible. In California, her father told her, he knew people with whom she could stay. People who would keep her safe from the kind of trouble she seemed sure to get into if she remained aboard the *White Swan*. He would leave her there while he went on to China, then pick her up on his return.

"No, Papa!" Tabitha cried when she heard this verdict. Tears welled in her blue eyes. "Please let me go to China with you—please. I've got my heart set on it."

But it wasn't the thought of missing China that caused Tabitha's tears. It was the thought of being separated from Tom, just when she had begun to realize how much he meant to her.

Chapter 12

TABITHA AND TOM WERE KEPT FAR APART—CAPTAIN Walker saw to that. The *White Swan* sailed in to Bodega Bay a week later, passing, on its way, an island of seals just like the one Snowball had fled to.

"I'll wager Snowball's made friends already," Captain Walker said, coming up behind his daughter at the rail. "Don't worry about leaving him behind, Tabitha."

She turned and looked at him. They'd barely spoken for a week. "You're treating me like a child, Papa," Tabitha said. The look in her blue eyes almost broke her father's heart.

"Maybe," Captain Walker said. "But you *are* a child, Tabitha—my child. I'm just trying to protect you. The same way you tried to protect Snowball."

Tabitha glanced out toward the seal colony. "But I let him go, Papa. That was the thing. I let him go when it was time."

Captain Walker sighed. It was painful, this business

of raising a daughter. He tried to smile. "The dory's going ashore," he said. "Would you like to come with me?"

Tom was on dawn watch again, as he'd been all week, so Tabitha knew there was no hope of talking to him today. Nodding, she accepted her father's invitation. There would be time enough to talk to Tom later, she thought. Perhaps the two of them could think of some way to make her father change his mind about leaving her in California.

Tabitha's worries evaporated like mist as the dory was rowed to shore. Before her was California and Bodega Bay. There were ships—four-masters, schooners, sloops—more ships than she had ever seen in any one place at any one time.

Some ships were berthed by wharves, others were anchored out in the bay. Tabitha could make out a few stores and buildings close to the shore line, and behind them, stretching up to the sky, were mountains. The Pacific Ocean at her feet, and mountains in the distance—it took her breath away.

Once on land Tabitha stayed close to her father's side—the wharves and the one dirt road that ran beside them were crowded with people. And such people! Tabitha heard a strange language spoken by tall, mustached men wearing elaborate fur hats.

"Russian," her father said, "they're from Russia. They've come down from Sitka, Alaska, to trade furs."

Then there were the men wearing short black jackets, narrow black trousers, and frilly sleeved shirts—

Tabitha couldn't understand what they were saying, either.

"They're speaking Spanish," her father told her. "They're the descendants of the people who originally settled in California."

"And look at the men in those funny robes with the hoods—"

"Monks," her father said. "There are a number of missions all up and down the California coast."

There was still more—stocky men, mostly blond, speaking a language that was neither Russian nor Spanish.

"There's a settlement of Swiss nearby," Captain Walker said, "and they speak a form of German."

Tabitha didn't know where to look first: at the people, the scenery, the shop windows that held many objects she had never seen before.

"It's fabulous," she said, thinking, *if only Tom were here to see it with me*.

"I think you'll like California, Tabitha," her father said, "and I know my friend, Don Felipe Alvarado will do his best to take care of you until I return." Captain Walker hesitated. Then, gently, he said, "I sent word we'd be there this afternoon."

Tabitha gasped. "This afternoon? But . . . but . . ." she bit her lip. "Can't I even say good-bye to Tom?"

"Good-byes are never pleasant," her father said. "You'll be able to say hello to him when we come back this way from China. That will give both of you some time to calm down. I want you to decide how you *really* feel, Tabitha."

But I know how I really feel! Tabitha's heart cried out. She glanced frantically out toward the bay where the *White Swan* lay at anchor. "What about my things?" she asked.

"Plum is putting them in your case. They'll be here with the next trip that the dory makes."

When the dory arrived it was Davy Pearson, of all people, who carried Tabitha's case ashore. "Good-bye, Davy," she said accusingly, as if he too had conspired in this.

"Good-bye, Tabitha," Davy replied coolly. Now that Tabitha was in disgrace with her father, Davy's attitude toward her had changed. He no longer saw her as a shortcut to inheriting a ship.

Tabitha glanced back at him. "Tell Tom I'll be waiting for him," she said stingingly. She turned on her heel with a toss of her head. So much for Davy Pearson. Someday she would tell Tom that he had been right about him all along.

Captain Walker hired a carriage and helped Tabitha inside. "We're going out to the Alvarado ranch," he told the driver.

Just like that, Tabitha thought, pressing her hands to her temples. *I'm being sent away from Tom just like that, without even a chance to say good-bye. Never mind—I'll see him again. I know I will.*

She clutched at one last fleeting hope. "How can you be so sure the Alvarados will take me?" she questioned. "They don't even know me."

Her father smiled, relieved to see that Tabitha was, at least, still talking to him. "This is California. People travel quite a distance to get here, and once they arrive they're expected to stay for a good long while. Besides, Californios are the most hospitable people in the world. The Alvarados will welcome you, Tabitha."

And, as they rode over the bumpy dirt roads, her father told her a little about his friends. Don Alvarado owned one of the largest ranches in that part of California, and he supplied much of the meat that was used on the ships traveling to the Orient. Tabitha's father brought him silks, teas, and jewels from China, and during the years they had traded together the two men had become good friends.

"And Don Alvarado has a daughter close to your age," Captain Walker said. "Ines—I guess she's seventeen, or thereabouts. He's got a son, too, Juan—he's a couple of years older. I'm sure you and Ines will get along just fine."

I just bet we will, Tabitha thought, picturing her own small house in New Bedford. She hoped there would be a guest room—no matter how small—or she and this Ines person would end up sharing the same room. Ines didn't even know her, and she was bound to feel put out if she had to share her room with a stranger.

"Here we are," her father said.

"Here we are? Where?" Tabitha looked around and she didn't see anything, just more land with the mountains still in the distance.

"You see that gate?" her father said, pointing. "That's the beginning of Don Alvarado's ranch."

Tabitha saw a tall iron gate, with the letters *F* and *A* elaborately intertwined out of wrought iron at the top, but as far as she could see, it was a gate that led to nowhere except to the dirt road on the other side of it—and that didn't seem to lead anywhere, either.

"Don't they even have a house?" Tabitha asked. She thought of the comfortable white house she had left back home. "What do they do? Live in a tent?"

Her father smiled but said nothing, and they rode in silence for another half hour or so when Tabitha finally saw a little house in the distance.

She was relieved, but she didn't understand the Alvarados. "Why did they put their house at the very end of their ranch? It doesn't make sense."

"It's not the end of the ranch, Tabitha," her father said, "it's the middle. This is all Alvarado land—as far as the eye can see."

Tabitha looked about her—the Alvarado ranch was huge! It looked big enough to hold the entire town of New Bedford.

As they drove closer, Tabitha could see that what she took for a *little* house was really quite large. The walls were of some white substance, and the roofs were of curved red tiles. And there were several roofs, Tabitha realized, as wing after wing of the house stretched out in four directions. It was really the biggest house she had ever seen, and Tabitha self-consciously smoothed down her white cotton dress with the little green sprigs. She tied her straw bonnet straighter on her head, but she still didn't feel entirely comfortable. "I'm not going to make a very good impression," she said sullenly. "I hope you know that."

"You look fine, Daughter," her father reassured her. He turned in the carriage seat and took another look at her. "As a matter of fact, for a young lady who's traveled all the way from Massachusetts, you look remarkable."

But Tabitha didn't feel remarkable, especially when the entire Alvarado family gathered on the wide, covered verandah to greet the Walkers.

"My friend," Don Alvarado said, and he actually embraced her father.

Well, you'd never see that back in New Bedford, Tabitha thought.

Captain Walker introduced his daughter, and Tabitha could see that her father had been right about one thing—Don Alvarado welcomed her as though she were his own long lost daughter.

"My house is your house," he said. "It is a great honor and pleasure to meet the daughter of my good friend, *Capitan* Walker."

He then introduced his daughter and son. Tabitha's eyes widened: Ines had hair dark as a blackbird's wing, and it was pulled back into a sleek bun at the back of her neck. She was wearing clothes the likes of which Tabitha had never seen before: a black wool skirt—except that it wasn't a skirt at all, it was really a pair of pants that were so full they looked like a skirt. Ines had on a snowy white shirt, topped by a waist-length black jacket, and her legs were encased in the shiniest black leather boots Tabitha had ever seen. She decided right then and there that Ines was just the most elegant girl she had ever seen.

But Ines actually apologized for her outfit. "You will excuse me for greeting you this way," she said, "but I have been out riding."

That was Ines, and Tabitha could hardly speak when she came face to face with Juan Alvarado. Her father had said he was about nineteen, but that was *all* he had said. He had forgotten to mention that Juan was tall and slim, and that in black riding clothes he looked both dashing and dangerous—except when he smiled, of course. Then his white teeth flashing against his tanned skin made his face light up like a desert sun rise.

"I, too, have been riding," he said, pretending that the speck or so of dust on his boots made him not quite fit to be seen. "I shall change immediately now that we are honored with such a beautiful guest."

Tabitha blushed as Juan's bold eyes rested on her. Like the other Alvarados, he spoke English out of courtesy to her, but the rich, Spanish accents were still in his voice.

"Of course you will stay with us," Ines said. Acting as hostess for her father, Ines took Tabitha's hand. "Can I show you to your room?" she asked. "Perhaps you wish to change before lunch."

Tabitha wished that she could change into clothes that were better than anything she owned. She followed Ines into the large, cool house, realizing that everything her father had said about the Alvarados was absolutely true. They were warm and welcoming, and they seemed to take it for granted that Tabitha would be their guest for as long as she wished to stay—even if that was forever. As sore and aching as her heart was over Tom, the Alvarados' kindness soothed it.

Tabitha followed Ines down a wide corridor that was floored in shiny terra cotta tile. Ines led her into a room that Tabitha saw was larger than the whole front room of the Byrd house in New Bedford. "I hope you will be comfortable here," Ines said. "We must seem primitive to someone who comes from the United States."

"But aren't you part of the United States too?" Tabitha asked. Her knowledge of geography was sketchy.

Ines' rich laugh echoed through the room. "Do not ask my father that," she replied. "It is a very big topic right now. California is independent in spirit, but a territory of Mexico in reality. My father and his friends wish it to become truly independent. But California is a rich prize. Mexico wishes to keep us. The United States wishes to take us from them, and also the Russians. There is much talk of fighting."

Tabitha looked around at the snowy-white, hand-crocheted bedspread, at the chests that were beautifully carved out of dark wood, and at the bright red and orange rug next to the ornately carved bed. Everything was peace and tranquility. "There won't be fighting, will there?" Tabitha asked.

Ines shrugged. "Who knows? Who ever knows what a sunrise may bring?"

Who knew indeed? Tabitha wondered. It wasn't so long ago that she had been standing on the deck of the *White Swan,* safe and secure in Tom's arms. Today she was here in this room, with Tom miles away. Who knew which way their futures would take them?

Chapter 13

THE NEXT FEW DAYS WERE FILLED WITH NEW AND exciting things. That was fortunate, for it helped keep Tabitha's mind from dwelling too much on Tom Howard or the *White Swan*, both on their way to China without her. Even so, there were moments when Tabitha was silent and brooding, and this was a source of sadness to her generous hosts.

"Why don't we go visiting?" Ines suggested one afternoon. "The Ortega ranch isn't far away—only about twenty miles. One of the hands could accompany us."

Tabitha looked down at her dress. All of her clothes had grown shabby during their months at sea. On board she hadn't noticed them. But, in the splendor of the Alvarado home, they were miserably noticeable. She couldn't embarrass her hosts by going visiting in rags.

"I don't have the right clothes, Ines," Tabitha said. "I should have asked Papa to leave money for some."

"But you must wear some of my things," Ines said, as she led Tabitha into her bedroom. She flung wide the doors of the wardrobe that ran the length of the large room. "Please—help yourself to anything that you find good enough—"

"Good enough! I couldn't take your clothes, Ines, they're *too* good."

Ines laughed. "But I have so much," she said. "Papa's family sends things from Spain, Mama's family sends things from Mexico. If I were to change my clothes three times a day, I still would have too much. You understand—you probably left a wardrobe full of clothes in your home."

"Not really," Tabitha said honestly, thinking of the economy that had prevailed in Aunt Priscilla's home. "I didn't have that much to begin with. Ines, you mentioned your mother—is she in Mexico now?"

Ines shook her head. "My mother died some years ago, Tabitha. That is why I try to run this house for my father the way she would have done it."

"You're lucky to have your father," Tabitha said, feeling sad. "My mother's dead too, but I hardly know my father. He's been at sea most of my life. I thought I'd get to know him on this trip. But, somehow, I feel I know him even less."

Ines smiled sympathetically. "He probably feels the same way about you, Tabitha. Fathers and daughters can sometimes be a great mystery to each other. But he will come back again, no? And he will be so glad to see you that everything between you will be forgotten."

Like the rest of the Alvarado family, Ines knew that Tabitha had been put ashore for some misbehavior. Politely, she did not pry into what that misbehavior might be. Instead, she tried to turn the conversation to a happier topic. Reaching into the wardrobe, she took out a pale green dress. "Look at this—silk, and it will be beautiful with your dark red hair."

Tabitha held the dress up against her and looked into the mirror. "It's a beautiful dress, Ines."

She could not help wondering how Tom would like her in her new dress—not that he would see her in it, she quickly reminded herself. Tom was on his way to China by now. Why couldn't she shake the feeling that he was somewhere nearby?

Ines wasn't the only one who noticed Tabitha's drooping spirits. Don Alvarado noticed also, and one night at dinner he commanded, "Ines, Juan—you must plan some entertainments to amuse our guest."

"Of course," Juan agreed quickly, looking up. "Tomorrow we'll take you riding to Crystal Springs waterfall, Tabitha. It's a beautiful place, and one of the original missions built by the Franciscan fathers is nearby."

"But I don't know how to ride," Tabitha said.

Juan laughed. "Is that all? I'll teach you. One or two lessons and you'll be riding like a *charro*."

"A *charro?*" Tabitha was interested in spite of herself. "What's that?"

"Our cowboys—our *vaqueros*," Juan explained. "They put on their fanciest riding clothes on Sundays and do all kinds of tricks—riding, roping—then they're called *charros*."

Tabitha looked up at Juan. He was a good-looking

young man, and good-looking in a way that was completely new to her. He was nineteen, but he seemed a lot older—more in charge, somehow.

"I'd like to learn to ride," Tabitha said. "We don't do much of that back in New Bedford."

"We all ride here," Ines said. "Come, let's go upstairs—you can try on some of my riding clothes."

"I've already borrowed so many of your clothes, Ines," Tabitha protested. "It isn't right."

"Never mind," Ines said. "If I ever get to New Bedford, you can lend me your . . . your fishing clothes?"

Tabitha laughed, picturing exotic Ines wearing an oilcloth coat and boots. "Oh, Ines," she cried between bursts of laughter. It felt good.

"But isn't that what you do in New Bedford? Go fishing?"

Tabitha shook her head. "Only the men do that, Ines. They go out on ships and are gone for months—sometimes years—depending on whether they're going after fish or whales."

"I wouldn't like that," Ines said, as she laid an assortment of riding clothes on her bed, "life without men—it must be lonely, and *boring*."

"*Eyeah*," Tabitha said, remembering the endless pacing on the widows' walks of New Bedford. Suddenly, she realized she had given the New England version of the word "yes." She laughed again, this time at herself. "I guess I'm more of a New Englander than I thought. But I'm willing to become a . . . a . . . what's the word, Ines?"

"Californio?"

"That's it," Tabitha responded, setting her jaw. "A Californio. Do you and Juan really think you can teach me to ride?"

"*Sin duda,*" Ines replied, her black eyes sparkling.

"What's that mean?"

"Without a doubt," Ines informed her.

"*Sin duda,*" Tabitha repeated. "Without a doubt. I like that."

She borrowed one of Ines' divided skirts, a white shirt with a foam of lace at the throat, and a short leather jacket. Ines showed her how to pull her hair back into a coil, and Tabitha studied her reflection in the mirror.

"You see," Ines said. "You look like one of us already."

Tabitha tried to remember the complicated things Ines had told her about California's political status. "That would make me a citizen of Mexico, right?" she asked. If she was going to live here until the *White Swan* returned, she ought at least to know something about where she was living.

"Never say so around my father, Tabitha. I have warned you—he is most touchy about this topic. We are citizens of Mexico in name only. My father, and many others like him, believe that soon we will be an independent country."

"And what am I around your father, then?" Tabitha asked.

"A citizen of California," Ines replied.

Tabitha smiled. "*Sin duda,*" she replied. She very

much liked the idea of being among people to whom independence mattered.

"Shall we go now?" Ines asked. "I see Juan out in the yard waiting for us." Tabitha nodded and Ines paused to look at her with deep black eyes. "I would so like for you to get to know my brother, Tabitha. He seems a little, well, stern, at times, but he is sweet beneath. And he likes you—I know he does."

Tabitha didn't reply. She hadn't told Ines about Tom and she wasn't prepared to—not yet, anyway. "I'm sure your brother is nice, Ines," she replied as they descended the stairs.

And Juan was nice. Tabitha saw that during the next few days while he gave her riding lessons on Belleza, a gentle black mare from the Alvarado stables.

"Lace the reins between these fingers," Juan said gently, wrapping the reins around Tabitha's hands. He paused. "But you must always wear gloves, Tabitha, or the reins will cut into your hands."

"Oh, gloves," said Tabitha, who tended to lose at least one each time she wore a pair. "They're such a nuisance. You don't wear them yourself, Juan."

"I'm a man," Juan said. "It's all right if I get calluses on the palms of my hands. Put on your gloves. Didn't Ines give you a pair?"

"Yes, yes, she did."

Juan waited until Tabitha slipped on the gloves before he would go on with the lesson.

"Back straight," he instructed. "Sit *up*, Tabitha! Sit *up*."

Tabitha rode around in the careful circle that Juan

had indicated, and she thought she was doing just fine, until she heard: "Heels *down,* Tabitha. Yes, like that—that's wonderful. Don't forget—heels *down,* back *straight.*"

Tabitha held a riding crop in her right hand, and sometimes she yearned to use it on Juan. Who cared whether her heels were up or down? What difference did it make? But just as she was about to say that she didn't care if she never learned to ride, Juan would turn his dazzling smile on her.

"That's wonderful, Tabitha, wonderful! For a girl who's never ridden before, you're learning very fast. And," his voice dropped, and he came closer to her side, "you look more beautiful on a horse than any girl I've ever known. Some Sunday soon you'll be riding with the *charros.*"

Tabitha looked at Juan, who was standing beside her left stirruped foot, waiting to help her off Belleza. He grinned up at her, and she felt his strong hand at her waist as he helped her out of the saddle.

"I make you angry sometimes, don't I, *querida?*" Juan asked. "But some things can't be taught with soft words."

His question was lost on Tabitha, who was trying to figure out what the word *querida* meant. Later on, as they were going down to dinner, she asked Ines to explain it to her.

Ines smiled faintly. "It can mean *dear* or it can mean *darling,* it's all in the way it's said. Your father could say *querida* to you, and so could a boy who really likes you. How did Juan sound when he said it, Tabitha?"

Tabitha blushed. Well, of course Ines would guess that it was her brother who had spoken that word. Who else could it have been? "He sounded like someone talking to a dumb girl. I think he was trying to make me feel a little better after he'd been yelling at me for close to an hour."

Ines shook her head. "Juan didn't yell, Tabitha. I would have heard him if he had yelled, because when Juan yells you can hear him all over the ranch."

"Not yell, exactly," Tabitha admitted. "Scold is more like it—'back straight, Tabitha, heels down, Tabitha.' Do you think I'll ever be able to ride well enough to *go* somewhere? I'm awfully tired of riding around in circles."

"Soon," Ines promised, "and probably sooner than you think."

Tabitha didn't know if Ines repeated her complaint to Juan, but the next morning brother and sister were waiting with the good news: Juan felt that Tabitha had progressed enough for the three of them to go to Crystal Springs together.

"At last," Tabitha said gleefully, "at last!"

They mounted up after breakfast, and with Ines and Juan on either side of Tabitha, they took a road away from the ranch—a rocky road that led up into the mountains.

At one point, when the road curved steeply, Ines rode ahead and Juan remained at Tabitha's side. Belleza stumbled slightly as a small pile of stones became dislodged by a front hoof, and for a second Tabitha was afraid that both she and her horse would go down.

But Juan's hand covered hers, and he helped her pull up on the reins. Now there was no scolding, no "pull up, Tabitha"; instead there was his strong, sure hand, and a softly spoken, "Don't be afraid, *querida,* I'm right here. Come on, Belleza." He gave a whistle that was clearly familiar to the little black mare. "Behave yourself!"

The mare's head went up, and they went on as before, except that Tabitha had heard *querida* once again. How did it sound? She wasn't sure. Was it *dear?* Was it *darling?* It was hard enough to tell what a boy meant when he was speaking English, but when he was speaking Spanish, it was totally beyond her.

The road took one more abrupt turn, and then they were facing the most beautiful sight Tabitha had ever seen. Falling from the top of a tall, granite needle of a mountain was a crystal-clear waterfall. It splashed into a pool with green and grassy banks, the green almost completely hidden by masses of the deepest purple violet-like flowers that Tabitha had ever seen.

Tabitha gasped, "Oh, it's so beautiful!" Her eyes filled with tears, and Juan and Ines were sure that their friend was moved at the sight of such loveliness. But the clear water and the flowers had reminded Tabitha of another day—of a picnic beside another stream where there had been violets.

Oh, Tom, she thought with a pang, *I miss you so much. If only you were here with me now! How will I ever wait until you come back?*

Chapter 14

TABITHA'S RIDING WAS PROGRESSING QUICKLY, AND Juan was extremely proud of her.

"Would you like to ride with us this Sunday?" he asked her one evening as they sat on the wide verandah. The *charro* riding, held every week, was to be at the nearby village of Santa Margarita.

"Oh, it would be wonderful for you to ride with us," Ines cried enthusiastically. "We all get dressed up in riding clothes decorated with silver braid and silver buttons. Have I showed you my outfit? I have three of them, so I will give you one." Ines' eyes sparkled. "There's nothing like it back in New Bedford, I bet."

Tabitha laughed. "I'm sure there isn't. What's it like? The riding, I mean?"

"Well, we ride in the arena with our *vaqueros*—all the ranch owners do that. Only now that Juan and I are grown, we are the ones who ride, instead of our father. It's like a team."

Tabitha's eyes gleamed. It did sound like fun.

"Will you ride with us, Tabitha?" Juan asked.

"Absolutely," Tabitha replied, brushing back a sweep of red hair.

"There's lots of noise and music," Ines warned. "Sometimes the horses get skittish. You won't be afraid?"

"I won't be afraid," Tabitha replied.

Juan looked at her approvingly. He liked Tabitha more and more. She fit into California life beautifully, he thought. She could stay here forever, as far as he was concerned. He reached out and brushed her shoulder with his hand. "Even if you are afraid," he said caressingly, "I'll be right beside you, *querida*."

Tabitha saw Ines smile, and she realized that her friend thought she was doing all this to make herself more attractive to her brother, when the truth was that she really wanted to go *charro* riding. If only Ines knew the truth—knew that her heart lay a thousand miles away or more, on a boat that was heading toward China.

On Sunday morning Ines helped Tabitha dress in a true *charro* outfit: a black divided skirt, snowy white shirt trimmed with lace, a short, fitted black jacket, and a flat-crowned black hat.

At first Tabitha thought it was a lot of black—until she saw the silver braid that edged the jacket and the sides of the skirt, and the silver buttons that decorated the entire costume.

Mounted on Belleza, with Juan and Ines on either side of her, Tabitha rode into the small, dusty arena of

Santa Margarita. Behind them rode the *vaqueros* from the Alvarado ranch—all forty of them—dressed in *charro* outfits that were even more splendid. Their hats were the wide-brimmed, high-crowned hats of the legendary Mexican *vaqueros*, decorated with loopings of silver braid that sparkled in the sunlight.

Every ranch tried to send its best, most spectacular-looking riders to the Sunday morning riding festival, and that morning the onlookers agreed that the riders from the Alvarado ranch stole the show. Between the two black-haired Alvarados, Tabitha burned like a radiant flame.

"Look at that red-haired beauty," Tabitha heard someone say as she passed a group of men.

The *mariachi* band played a loud trumpet fanfare as the Alvarados rode around the arena, and Belleza began to prance.

"Are you all right?" Juan asked, ready to help Tabitha if help was needed.

"I'm just fine," Tabitha said, and her dark blue eyes flashed. "Don't help me with the reins, Juan. No need for anyone to know that I've only just learned to ride."

Juan threw his head back and laughed. "You are wonderful, Tabitha. Don't worry, I won't touch the reins. I don't have to—you're doing fine."

Tabitha hoped she was doing fine. She was getting more accustomed to Belleza's ways each time she went riding, and now she could tell that Belleza was getting nervous and skittish. "It's all right," she said, patting the horse's neck with one gloved hand, "don't you be afraid, Belleza. Remember, you've got to perform, too."

Belleza responded to Tabitha's touch, shook her black-maned head, and walked more calmly.

Juan heard Tabitha, and he turned slightly in his saddle to look at her. She was the kind of girl any man could be proud of, he thought as he gazed at her. The Alvarados and Tabitha circled the arena one more time. Then they dismounted and took their seats to watch the other *charros* perform.

"I am proud of you, Tabitha," Juan said.

"I do ride pretty well, don't I?" Tabitha asked saucily.

"Not *pretty* well—*very* well," he told her, and he squeezed her hand—a gesture that Tabitha convinced herself was nothing more than a brotherly show of affection.

Dinner was always an event in the Alvarado household, and that night's dinner, to honor Tabitha's debut as a *charro*, was especially elaborate.

As she struggled to get the pearl buttons right on her dress, Tabitha remembered dinners in New Bedford. Back home people only dressed up when they were invited to a party—not to sit around a table and eat supper with family. But she enjoyed it, enjoyed sweeping down to dinner every night as if it *were* a party, enjoyed feeling beautiful when the approving eyes of the Alvarado men swept over her. Everything here was strange and exotic and delightful, even the food that was served. "This is just delicious," Tabitha said to Ines as she tasted her soup. "I've never had anything like it before. What is it?"

"It's corn and tortilla soup," Ines replied.

"Tortilla? Oh, I remember—they're those funny-looking pancakes we had yesterday." She glanced at Don Alvarado and saw, for the first time, that he was frowning. "Funny-looking—but delicious," she added quickly.

Don Alvarado's face remained set in a frown. Tabitha exchanged glances with Ines, who motioned her to remain silent. But Tabitha had never been one to heed such warnings. "Is something wrong, Don Alvarado?" she asked.

"Wrong?" he said, his brows lowering like storm clouds. "Wrong? Only enemies—howling wolves—at our door, that is all."

"What—?" Tabitha began, but Ines silenced her with a quickly whispered warning.

Now it was Juan's turn to question Don Alvarado. "Where were you this afternoon, Father? Where did you go during the *charro* riding?"

"To Fort Ross," he said, spitting out the words as if they were bitter pills. "I saw Baron von Wrangell there."

"The Russian envoy?" Juan asked, and his father nodded.

Now Tabitha began to guess why Don Alvarado was in such a terrible mood. It must have something to do with California, with his desire to see California free and independent.

"The news is not good for us Californios," Don

Alvarado said, and Tabitha felt a tightening in her stomach. "The Russian baron has been talking with the minister from Mexico City." Don Alvarado's fist crashed suddenly onto the white tablecloth. "Mexico wants Russia as an ally! And to make the deal, we may be the bait."

Juan looked at his father. "What do you mean, Father?" he asked. The silence in the Alvarado dining room was as thick as the corn and tortilla soup, which everyone had stopped eating.

"It means," Don Alvarado said with barely controlled anger, "it means that to get the Russians as an ally, Mexico may give us—give California!—to them."

"*Give* California to the Russians?" Tabitha asked, unable to remain silent. "How can anyone *give* other people away? It isn't right."

Don Alvarado looked at her. "That is how I hoped Americans would feel," he said. "After all, your country has fought for independence. Might not your countrymen understand that independence is equally important to us?"

"Of course they will," Tabitha cried.

"You are a child, Tabitha. That is not how the hearts of men work. They understand only power and money. Why, just today, at Fort Ross, I saw an American in league with the Russians. He was working for the fur traders who'd come down from Sitka, lining his pockets at our expense."

Tabitha felt her cheeks burn. "But how do you know the man you saw was American?" she asked hotly.

"Baron von Wrangell told me so himself."

"But he could have been wrong," Tabitha persisted. "You said yourself the Russians are your enemies—maybe he was just making up a story—"

"It is fine that you are so patriotic," Don Alvarado said, "but that boy was tall as only Americans are tall, and so blond his hair was almost white. And when he spoke, it was English—*American* English. No, he was American, all right, and working with the Russians."

Tabitha's spoon clattered to her plate. A tall blond boy . . . hair almost white . . . there was only one boy she had ever met who fit that description—Tom Howard. But how could it be? How could Tom be at Fort Ross, and what on earth would he be doing working for the Russians?

"Tabitha." It was Ines' voice, coming to her through the warm silence. "Tabitha, what's wrong? Are you all right?"

Tabitha opened her eyes. The whole world had changed. "Yes," she said, "I'm fine. It's just a little warm in here, I guess. And I'm not quite used to talking politics."

Don Alvarado smiled. "My apologies, *señorita.* I forget, sometimes, that you are not my own child. The worries of California are not your concern."

But Don Alvarado was wrong. If California hadn't been her concern before, it certainly was now.

Chapter 15

IT WAS TWO DAYS AFTER SUNDAY'S RIDING EVENT that Tabitha proposed something daring to Ines. At least Ines thought it was daring, though it didn't seem so much to Tabitha.

"Ride to Fort Ross?" Ines asked. "Just the two of us? Can't we take Domingo with us? He's the *vaquero* that usually rides with me when Juan and Papa do not have the time."

But Tabitha didn't want to ask Domingo to accompany them. He would be sure to mention the trip to Juan or to Don Alvarado, and that might be the end of everything.

"Why do we need Domingo?" Tabitha asked. "Why do we need anyone? You're a marvelous rider, Ines, and I'm doing all right on Belleza."

"It isn't the riding," Ines said, biting her lip. "It's Fort Ross—I've never been there alone, without an escort. It wouldn't be right."

But Tabitha was determined to wear Ines down. "What's so scary about Fort Ross?" Tabitha asked. "Who's there?"

"Men," Ines said innocently. Like a beautiful desert flower, Ines had been protected by her father and brother. "There are all kinds of rough men there, Tabitha," Ines continued, "men from every strange place in the world—Russians, Indians, Portuguese, and those men from the trading ships who come from just about everywhere. We can't go there alone, Tabitha."

Tabitha sighed. Ines would be even more against the plan if she knew that seeing one of those men—a tall sailor with star-white hair—was exactly why she wanted to go to Fort Ross. She tried a different approach.

"All right, Ines. But can we at least go riding? Just the two of us? There's nothing wrong with that, is there?"

"I suppose not," Ines said, but she sounded doubtful. Before she could mount a protest, Tabitha pulled her out to the stables and had two horses saddled.

Once the two were riding among the sloping hills and live oaks, Ines began to lay aside her doubts. Tabitha encouraged her by saying, "See how much fun breaking the rules can be?"

Ines nodded. "I've never done anything like this before," Ines replied. "My father and Juan have gone to buy cattle—if they were here we could never do this, Tabitha."

"We'll be back before they know we're gone," Tabitha assured her, wondering how she was going to persuade Ines to ride with her all the way to Fort Ross.

It turned out to be easier than she thought. As they

rode along, Tabitha told Ines about how she had hidden on the *White Swan*, and she told her about the Falkland Islands, and about Snowball. She told her about everything and everyone *except* Tom Howard. Tabitha's adventures made Ines feel she was missing something, and then Tabitha said, "We've come this far, Ines, why don't we just go on and ride to Fort Ross? It isn't much further, is it?"

"It's not far at all, Tabitha. You're right—why shouldn't we ride to Fort Ross? We'll just ride through the town—we won't talk to anyone."

"Unless we see someone we know," Tabitha said.

"What?"

"And there's not much chance of that, is there?"

"Of course there isn't," Ines answered. And the two girls spurred their horses and rode at a canter to the edge of the busy settlement called Fort Ross.

It wasn't a fort at all, Tabitha saw with a sense of mounting excitement. At least not a fort in the military sense. There were no platoons of soldiers, no parade grounds and no barracks. Instead, there was a lively, bustling trading settlement. And trading was something that Tabitha, the daughter of a merchant and seafaring family, understood very well. It caused a kind of throbbing in her blood, and for a moment it made Tabitha forget everything else. Voices in four or five different languages drowned each other out as merchants offered their wares—strings of beads, laces, gloves, ribbons of silk—to the two pretty young women.

"Oh!" cried Tabitha. "Ines, look at that! What's it

called?" She was admiring a hand-woven cloak of brilliantly varied colors. At a nod from Tabitha, the Mexican merchant quickly helped her dismount.

Ines had begun to grow alarmed. "Tabitha," she said reprovingly, sliding down from her own mount, "you said we would only ride through. You said we would talk to no one."

"But Ines—"

Tabitha's words were lost. Suddenly, Ines let out a piercing scream of alarm. Tabitha whirled around and saw a large, dark-bearded seaman holding onto Ines' arm.

"Come to do a little sight-seeing, have you?" the seaman asked. He was wearing dirty white pants and his jacket was torn. "Why, I'll be happy to show you around, two pretty things like you."

Ines looked at Tabitha with helpless eyes. Tabitha turned on the seaman. "Let go of her this instant!" she said icily.

"Oh, so you're a jealous one, eh, missy?" the seaman grinned. He released his hold on Ines and grasped Tabitha's hand instead. "Well, now, I'm not partic'lar, so long's I've got my hands on a pretty girl!"

Tabitha brought her free hand up to the sailor's face, fingers curled like talons. She raked her nails across his cheek and the sailor shrieked in pain. Releasing her, he looked at Tabitha with blazing eyes. "Little wildcat you are. Well, you'll pay for that, I'll be bound you will!"

A crowd had gathered around them, but no one had stepped forward to help the girls. The sailor, apparently, was a notorious bully, with a long and evil reputation at Fort Ross. Tabitha felt a tremor of fear as he looked at her with fierce eyes, rubbing his raw cheek and repeating, "Aye, you'll pay for that, my miss."

But now there was a ripple in the air as the crowd parted. A very tall, very blond young man stepped into the circle and stared at the big sailor. Tabitha's heart stopped in her chest.

"I'll settle the ladies' debts for them," Tom Howard said. Tabitha was behind him. She saw the muscles in his back flex as he cocked his fists.

The big sailor took Tom's measure and shrugged his huge shoulders. "Well, mate, if they're *your* ladies, well, you're welcome to 'em. Plenty of other lasses what'll be glad enough to put into port with Mike the Sailor."

And so saying, Mike the Sailor lurched off, rubbing his cheek. Tom turned to face Tabitha for the first time. It was like the sun coming up in front of her, taking her up into the dizzying air with it.

"I think," Tom said, closing the distance between them with a single long stride, "I think you owe me something, Tabitha."

Her blue eyes clouded with confusion. "Owe you? Well, thank you for stepping in like that, if that's what you mean," she said, not at all certain of her footing. Her mind buzzed and hummed with questions. What was Tom doing here? Why wasn't he on the *White Swan?* Was he really working for the Russians? Why? *Why?*

Now it was Tom's turn to look confused, but only for a second. "That's not exactly what I had in mind, Tabitha," he said. And right there, in front of the Mexican with the brightly colored capes, the astonished Ines, and half of Fort Ross, he swept her into his arms and kissed her. Hard. So hard it left her breathless. "Now *that's* what I had in mind," he said. His face broke into a slow grin. "That's my kiss for getting Snowball back into the boat that time, remember? I've been waiting all this time to collect it. I even jumped ship for it."

Tabitha searched his face, no longer caring who was watching them or what those watchers thought of her. "Oh, Tom," she said, her hands resting on the tops of his shoulders, her body swaying toward his as involuntarily as a blade of grass caught in a gust of wind, "is that really why you're here? Because of me?"

Tom pressed her close. "I couldn't sail on to China without seeing you, Tabitha. We wouldn't see each other for years. I had to know how you feel about me—about *us*. I've been looking all over this country for you, and asking everyone." He squeezed her. "I'd just about decided your father had put you on a whaler bound back for New Bedford."

Tabitha rested her stubborn chin on Tom's chest. "I told you, Tom, I'm not going back to New Bedford. Not for a while, at least."

"Your father's going to have my hide for jumping his

ship, you know, but I'm going to make it up to him. I'm going to prove I'm a good sailor and would make a good first mate on the *White Swan,* if it ever comes to that. But even if your father hates me forever, Tabitha, it's worth it." He stroked her hair, which seemed as warm as silk beneath his fingers. "It's worth it, just to see you."

"Tom," she said, her voice crumpling into a damp little ball. There was so much she wanted to tell him, so much she had come to realize in the past few weeks. But now there were no words, and all she could do was look into his eyes, those magical eyes that carried her out onto a sea of dreams.

Suddenly, she heard strange words around her, and the words broke through the golden web of her dream. A dark, mustached Russian dropped a pack of furs beside Tom and spoke a few words. Tom nodded in reply.

Tabitha looked at him searchingly. "You didn't join up with the Russians, did you, Tom?" she asked. "They want to control all of California, you know, and the Mexicans may let them have it."

Tom laughed. "Who've you been talking to, Tabitha? I didn't know you took such an interest in politics! But you don't have to worry—I haven't kicked in with the Russians. I'm just working for some of the traders who bring furs down from Sitka." He jerked his thumb at his companions. "These boys are about as political as a flock of sea gulls, if you want to know the truth."

Tabitha felt a great weight roll away from her heart.

At least she wouldn't have to worry about Tom and the Alvarados being on opposite sides anymore. "There sure are a lot of Russians here," Tabitha observed.

"There's a lot of all kinds of people here," Tom said. "Never saw so many foreigners in my life. But what're *you* doing here, Tabitha? That's what I've been wondering. And where have you been all these weeks? I looked everywhere but underneath the rocks out there."

The world began to come back to Tabitha. She remembered Don Alvarado, his ranch, Juan and Ines, her brief but splendid appearance as a *charro*. "Oh, Tom, I'll have to tell you all about it. I've learned to ride, Tom, really ride. So now I'll have to teach you."

"I learned too," Tom said, grinning. "Now we can go riding together, and—"

"Tabitha." It was Ines' voice, full of pleading urgency. Tabitha looked up and caught the alarm in Ines' full dark eyes. A second later she was looking at the black leather and magnificent silver spurs of Juan Alvarado's boots.

"What's going on?" Juan demanded, dismounting in one swift movement. Completely ignoring Tom, he turned angrily toward his sister and Tabitha. "What are the two of you doing here? Ines, you know well enough not to come to Fort Ross alone. What were you thinking of, bringing Tabitha here?"

"It wasn't her idea," Tabitha protested quickly. "It was mine. I made Ines do it, Juan."

She felt Tom stiffen at the easy way she spoke Juan's name. Why hadn't she hurried to explain things to him? Now he was probably thinking all sorts of wild things about her and Juan.

Juan was staring at Tabitha. "*Your* idea to come to Fort Ross, Tabitha? I do not think so. Fort Ross is only a name to you, no?"

Now Tom stepped up behind Tabitha, his hand resting possessively on her shoulder. "If Tabitha says it was her idea, it was her idea," he said challengingly.

Juan could no longer ignore Tom. "You will forgive me, *señor,*" he said between clenched teeth, his tone exaggeratedly polite, "but Tabitha is now living on our ranch, at the request of her father. She is my responsibility." He turned his head aside. "Tabitha, Ines, get on your horses."

"Now just a minute there," Tom shouted, facing Juan Alvarado. "I haven't heard Tabitha say that she wants to go anywhere with you."

"Tom, Juan—please—" Tabitha whispered, not moving a foot.

Ines, obediently, was already on her horse. "Juan," she pleaded, "Father will be furious if you have a fight on the streets of Fort Ross!"

But it didn't look to Tabitha as though Juan cared how angry his father would be—he was so angry himself. Tom had challenged his pride and his authority and, perhaps, touched a chord of jealousy as well, for Juan had seen how Tabitha returned Tom's smiles and his touches.

It was the appearance of a man in a uniform more elaborate than any Tabitha had ever seen that finally stopped Tom and Juan from going further.

The man saluted Juan casually, as if they were old friends. "*Señor* Alvarado," he said respectfully, "is there any trouble?"

With a start, Tabitha realized that the uniformed man was the marshal of the settlement. One word from Juan could put Tom behind bars. She looked at Juan with pleading eyes.

Tabitha didn't know if her silent message got through or not, but after a moment Juan took a deep breath and said, "No trouble, Jefe—no trouble that I cannot handle myself."

"That is just it, *Señor* Alvarado," the man said quietly. "There is no need for you to handle trouble in Fort Ross by yourself. If this man is giving you any trouble—" he indicated Tom, "—I will put him in jail."

Juan looked at Tom and then at Tabitha. "It is a personal thing, Jefe," he said, "there is no need to arrest this man on my account."

Tabitha breathed a sigh of relief, and this time when Juan said, "Get on your horse, Tabitha," she was quick to obey him.

"But Tabitha—" Tom said, "Tabitha—"

"Not now, Tom," Tabitha whispered, wishing there was time to whisper to Tom all the things that were in her heart. "Not now." And she turned Belleza's head and rode after Ines.

Chapter 16

"INES, YOU HAVE BEHAVED DISGRACEFULLY." DON Felipe was speaking to both Ines and Tabitha, but he was pretending to address his remarks only to his daughter. "You know how you are expected to behave, even though other people do not—"

"Don Alvarado—" Tabitha tried to interrupt him, but he pretended not to hear her.

"You have been brought up in California," Ines' father went on. "You know that no well-brought-up girl ever goes riding by herself—especially not to such a place as Fort Ross—"

"But Don Alvarado—"

"And then to stop on the street and talk to this renegade sailor—"

Tabitha wasn't sure what *renegade* meant, but she knew it couldn't be anything good. "Tom Howard is no renegade," she said staunchly.

But it didn't matter if she guessed the word's meaning correctly or not, because Don Felipe was still ignoring her.

"Everyone saw you, Ines. Everyone is talking about you—even those Russians—"

"But you don't like the Russians," Tabitha said, interrupting Don Alvarado for the fourth time, "so what difference does it make what they think?"

That was too much for Ines' father. "Tabitha, will you stop interrupting me!" he roared. Then he lowered his voice to a whisper and gave his attention back to his daughter. "How could you, Ines? Your behavior has broken my heart."

"Oh, Father," Ines said, tears sliding down her smooth olive skin.

"Don Alvarado, please." Tabitha tried to speak once again, and this time he turned his head and looked directly at her.

"Yes, Tabitha?" he said.

"It was my fault," Tabitha said quickly. "I *made* Ines come with me to Fort Ross. It was all my idea."

"Your idea or not," Don Felipe said coldly, "Ines should have known better."

"She couldn't let me go there by myself, could she?" Tabitha asked. "Wouldn't that have been worse? Ines really went because of me—she didn't want to let you down by letting me ride into Fort Ross all alone."

Tabitha wasn't sure if Don Felipe believed her, but he did seem to look a little more kindly at his daughter.

"Stop crying, Ines. Perhaps you were right—Tabitha is our responsibility. I promised my friend Captain Walker to take good care of his daughter." Here Don

Alvarado paused, and his dark eyes began to crackle once again. "But when you learned what this foolish girl wanted to do, you should have galloped back to the ranch for Domingo! For someone! You should never have ridden into Fort Ross by yourself, Ines!"

"She wasn't by herself, exactly," Tabitha said. "I was with her."

Don Felipe sighed. "We will not speak of this anymore."

Thank goodness, Tabitha thought.

"But Ines, you and Tabitha will not go riding again."

"Not ever?" Tabitha asked.

"Not for a long time," Don Felipe said. He felt a sense of comfort, as if the world were not, after all, beyond his control. "Not until I decide that the two of you know how to behave properly. Now go and get dressed for dinner."

"Can't we even go riding with Domingo?" Tabitha asked. "Or with Juan?"

"What makes you think I would take you riding again?" Juan asked sharply. He had many questions about the tall blond sailor, but Tabitha had made it clear that Tom Howard was her business and no one else's. Juan felt angry and rejected.

"Get dressed for dinner," Don Alvarado was roaring again. "I don't want to hear another word about riding!"

Now how was she going to talk to Tom? Tabitha wondered as she went to her room and took off her riding outfit. She had to explain to him about Juan—

that there was nothing between her and Juan and could never be. And she had to explain something else, too, something far more urgent.

Tom was in danger. He might not realize it, but he was. Just because *he* didn't think working with the Russians put him in their camp didn't mean everyone else thought so. Don Alvarado and the other Californios were sure to think of Tom as a Russian sympathizer, and if there was fighting . . . Tabitha closed her eyes. She had to think of some way to warn him. She had to.

The near-fight with Tom seemed to have brought all of Juan's romantic inclinations to the surface. After dinner, he took Tabitha walking beneath the big yellow moon. He took her hand in his.

"You must learn to be more careful, Tabitha," he scolded gently. "You do things, like going to Fort Ross, and do not think of the consequences. You just do as you wish, without thinking about the trouble you may get yourself into."

Tabitha sighed. Juan sounded a good deal like Aunt Priscilla back in New Bedford. "Are you sure you're just nineteen?" she couldn't resist asking.

Juan smiled. "Almost twenty," he answered. "Old enough to get married. Is that what you were thinking about, Tabitha, when you asked me about my age?"

Tabitha pulled her hand away from his in surprise. "Not at all," she said. She didn't dare tell him that she was thinking he sounded *too old* for nineteen or twenty.

Juan took her hand back. "But *I* was thinking about that, Tabitha." He brought her hand to his lips. "You and I, Tabitha, it could be a fine match, if you would just learn to act more properly."

Tabitha looked at him in alarm, glad that the shifting shadows of moonlight hid her true expression. "I . . . this is something I must think about, Juan," she said at last.

"You are right," Juan said apologetically, "I must speak to my father first, and then to your father. After they give their consent, it will be the proper time to ask you to be my wife." Thank goodness her father was on his way to China, Tabitha thought. "But, meanwhile," Juan went on, "it would be good if you learned more about our customs, Tabitha, learned to behave the way we do in California."

This annoyed Tabitha. Not once, in all the months she had spent with him aboard the *White Swan*, had Tom Howard attempted to tell her how to behave. "Do you think there's only one way to behave in California?"

"Only one *proper* way," Juan said, "and standing on the streets of Fort Ross talking to that sailor is not the proper way."

Tabitha yearned to see Tom, yearned to hear his open laughter, yearned to hear him say, "Let's go exploring, Tabitha." She could tell that Juan was not interested in exploring. He wasn't interested in trying new things or going to new places. Juan was nice—he had spent a lot of time teaching her to ride; he could have had Tom thrown into jail, but he hadn't. But she would never love him. Not in the way she loved Tom.

"I think I'd better go in now, Juan," Tabitha said, "it's been a long day."

"Good night, *querida,*" Juan said, bringing her hand to his lips again. This time there was no doubt at all about the way he meant *querida*. "I am glad we have had this little talk."

The moon was hanging low in the sky, illuminating the mountains in the far background. Tabitha put on her nightdress and got into bed. The dangers and confusions of the long day spun away from her. The moon made the quilted coverlet shine like silver. Everything in California was gold and silver, now that Tabitha knew Tom Howard was here.

It was dull not being allowed to go riding. Tabitha enjoyed riding around the countryside on Belleza, but Don Felipe's word was law, and he had insisted that Tabitha and Ines stay close to the ranch house.

If she couldn't go riding, the least she could do was pay Belleza a visit in her stall, and she went out one morning carrying lumps of sugar and an apple cut into quarters.

Domingo, the man in charge of the Alvarado stables, looked worried when he saw Tabitha—he was afraid that she would ask him to saddle Belleza for her. "I am sorry, *Señorita* Tabitha," he said, "but Don Felipe's orders—"

"I know, Domingo. I can't go riding—but I thought that Belleza might like some breakfast."

Domingo smiled sadly and left the stables.

After he had gone, Tabitha put the sugar on her palm, and Belleza happily took the offering. Then came an apple quarter, and Tabitha watched the horse munch away. The stable door opened behind her, but she didn't turn; it was probably Domingo again, or one of the other men come to clean out the stables.

"Just like in New Bedford," a voice at her shoulder said. "Remember the day of the picnic? I fed an apple to a horse—"

Tabitha whirled around. *"Tom!"* she cried, and her arms went automatically up around his neck, drawing him to her.

He bent to kiss her, then looked up, smiling as casually as though it was the most normal thing in the world for him to be in the Alvarado stables.

"Tom, what are you doing here? How did you find me?"

"I asked back at Fort Ross who that fellow was that rode off with you the other day. They told me, of course. Seems like all of California knows who the Alvarados are."

"That was Juan," Tabitha explained. "His father is a friend of my father's—that's why my father left me here. But—oh, never mind all that—I have so much to tell you." She paused, her eyes going from bright to dark. "You're in danger, Tom."

Tom grinned and looked around. "Funny," he said, tightening his arms around her. "I don't feel particularly threatened." He inhaled the fresh fragrance of her hair. "Matter of fact, I feel plumb comfortable."

Tabitha pulled away from him. "I don't mean *here*, Tom. I mean with the Russians."

Tom snorted. "I told you, Tabitha, I'm just working—"

"I know what you told me, Tom," Tabitha argued. "But it *looks* like you're in with them, that's the thing, and if there's any fighting over it—"

"Hey," Tom said, stopping her flow of words by resting his thumb firmly on her chin. "I can take care of myself. Besides, it's you I'm worried about."

"Me?" Tabitha asked.

"Sure. It was mighty surprising, Tabitha, the way you went along so easy with that Juan Alvarado. I didn't think you'd let anyone but your father tell you what to do—"

"You don't understand, Tom."

"No, he doesn't." Tom and Tabitha turned toward the new voice and saw Juan Alvarado's tall, lean form framed in the double door of the stable. He walked quickly to where they stood. "You will please leave my property, *señor.*"

His words were polite, but Tabitha could see that Juan was furious. He had a riding crop in his hand, and he raised it as he spoke.

Tom gently pushed Tabitha out of the way and faced Juan. "I don't have a buggy whip, but if that's what you need to fight, come on!"

Juan threw the riding crop down. "I don't need anything but my bare hands to throw you off my ranch!"

"Tom—Juan." Tabitha stepped between them. "Stop this—both of you!"

Tom faced Juan, his fists clenched. "I'll be happy to get off your ranch. I just came to get Tabitha."

Now Juan smiled, a cold and precise smile. "But that is what you do not understand, *señor,*" he said. "Tabitha is not leaving. She and I became engaged last night."

Tabitha felt the air go out of her lungs. Tom looked at her, but no words came to her lips. She just stood there, gasping for air.

"Tabitha?" Tom questioned. The pain in his eyes was more than she could bear to look at.

"Tom, I . . . I . . ."

"So you see, *señor,*" Juan said, coming between them, "you have no business here. None at all."

Tom Howard saw all his dreams vanish in Juan Alvarado's dark, self-assured smile. "You won't see me again, Tabitha," he said stiffly. He walked outside, closing the stable doors behind him, and in a few minutes Tabitha heard the clatter of horse's hooves.

The sound of the hooves brought her back to her senses. "What have you done?" she cried, turning on Juan with flashing eyes. "Oh, what have you *done?*"

Juan reached out to catch her arm but she tore away from him. She ran out of the stable.

"Tom," she cried out to him, "Tom—"

But he was already riding away. Tabitha watched him. As a child, she had read about hearts breaking, but back in New Bedford she had never known whether she had a heart to break or not. Now she knew. She felt her heart burst into lots of little pieces, like a mirror that would never again reflect the blue sky or soaring clouds.

Chapter 17

"BARON VON WRANGELL IS COMING TO DINNER TOnight," Don Alvarado told them at breakfast the next morning.

Tabitha sat in numb silence, scarcely believing what she had heard as Don Alvarado continued smoothly, "Ines, you will speak to Maria. We will have a very special dinner."

"Yes, Papa."

Even Juan was nodding calmly. Finally, Tabitha could no longer hold her tongue. "But the Russians are your enemies!" she exclaimed. "Why are they coming here to dinner, as if they were friends?"

Juan smiled at Tabitha. "The best way to see into an opponent's mind, Tabitha, is to gaze into his eyes."

He spoke clearly and with patience, but his meaning slipped away from Tabitha. Her brows drew together in confusion.

"What my son means," explained Don Alvarado, "is this. We want California to be independent. Right now we are a colony of Mexico. The Americans want us to be part of their country, the Russians want us to be part of theirs. But the dice—" he made a fist and shook his hand, as if rattling dice, "—the dice are in Mexico's hand." Here he paused and tossed his imaginary dice down the length of the table. "If they choose to give us to the Russians, we become theirs peaceably. But who's to say, eh? If they do not give us to the Russians, maybe the Russians will take us by force. Either way, I wish to know something of these strange big men. I wish them to trust me, at least enough to speak their hearts to me. Do you understand now, Tabitha?"

Tabitha nodded. Don Alvarado was a very wise man.

Here Juan took up the conversation again, traces of youthful pride in his voice. "Some of the other ranchers decided that we—the Alvarados—should talk to the Russians, find out just what their plans would be for California. If we can have more freedom with them than with the Mexicans, well then, so be it."

Tabitha looked quickly at Don Alvarado, who listened without saying more. Somehow, she didn't believe the matter was as simple as Juan believed it was. But if she ventured this opinion to him, he would no doubt tell her that girls had no understanding of politics.

Ines brightened at the idea of a dinner party. For years, ever since her mother's death, she had run the house and kept the china and crystal ready for guests. She loved showing guests how charming and comfortable her home was. That the guests usually cast admiring eyes at her as well was something Ines never thought of.

"I'll lend you my peach taffeta gown," she told Tabitha. "It will be dazzling with your hair."

"Peach? With my hair?" Tabitha, whose mind was far from gowns, was distracted nonetheless. "I don't think so, Ines."

Ines smiled her serene smile. "Trust me. You will look like a desert sunset. Let's see—the peach gown, your hair, and . . . hmm," she paused, her delicate finger tapping. "Yes, I know—the green lace shawl Uncle Felipe sent me for my birthday last year."

"Well," Tabitha conceded, "maybe." She wasn't sure, but decided that Ines might be right. She had never concerned herself too much about clothes, and she had no desire to argue.

Ines was right, and as Tabitha drifted down the length of the long table, searching for her place among the twenty place settings, she felt grateful to Ines for her concern. The dinner for the Russians *was* something special. The long dining table was set with a white embroidered cloth. Every napkin at each place was almost as big as a pillowcase, and the many candles on the table made the crystal goblets and the heavy silver gleam.

Tabitha felt nervous when she saw the row of forks at each place, and she hoped she wouldn't do anything to disgrace the Alvarados.

Tabitha at last found her place card. She was seated across from Ines but far from the Alvarado men, who sat near the top of the table. She was placed between two handsome young Russian noblemen, both of whom were named Alexei.

"But how shall I keep you straight?" Tabitha asked in carefully pronounced Spanish. She had been learning the language, a little at a time, from Juan and Ines, but this was the first time she had tested it on strangers.

"I am Alexei Ubetskoy, Baron von Wrangell's nephew," the Alexei on Tabitha's right said in heavily-accented Spanish.

"And I," said the Alexei on her left, "am Alexei—" and here he delivered a long and unpronounceable name that Tabitha could only shake her head at.

"No, no, no," she said, laughing. "I have a much better idea. *Alexei Uno, Alexei Dos.*" And so it was throughout the meal—Alexei One and Alexei Two. Tabitha glanced across the table to see what Ines was making of all this, but Ines was busy with Russians of her own. The one on her right was gazing into her eyes with rapt admiration. The one on her left was clowning for her attention.

And, at the head of the table, Baron von Wrangell was attempting to persuade Don Alvarado to share his own point of view. "Americans know precious little about ranching," was one of Baron von Wrangell's remarks. Tabitha silently wondered how that could be—even in New Bedford they had heard about the wonderful ranches in a territory called Texas.

"That is only one reason why I think, Don Alvarado," Baron von Wrangell said, "that you and your friends would feel much more at home with us—as a part of Russia. With our European background, European manners, European way of viewing the world, we could make something wonderful out of California."

"I think California already *is* wonderful," Don Alvarado said, but he didn't dispute the baron's idea that the Californios had more in common with the Russians than with the Americans.

Like Tabitha, the Alexeis had been straining to hear what was being said at the top of the table.

"A bit of Europe, a bit of civilization," said Alexei One, agreeing with his uncle, the baron. "That is what California could become."

"And the American women," Alexei Two said with a snort of laughter. "Have you seen them? So plain! So loud! Ugh! Can you imagine one of them at this table?"

Tabitha paused, fork frozen in midair, in shock. With a start she realized that Alexei Two, new to the Spanish language himself, had failed to recognize her accent. He had no idea that she was an American! And on her left, Alexei One laughed in agreement!

Tabitha felt her cheeks redden with anger. She looked across the table at Ines, but Ines was lost in a conversation of her own.

"Don't you agree, *señorita?*" Alexei One was asking.

"Agree about what?" Tabitha asked.

"That American women are far too loud? Perhaps it is because their men are weak!"

And this brought another burst of laughter from Alexei Two, who had started it all. Tabitha stood up suddenly. "Excuse me," she said, pushing her chair back from the table. *"Con su permiso."*

The two Alexeis stood up as she passed, then sat down again and continued with the conversation. As she walked down the corridor, Tabitha could still hear them laughing. It was the remark about American men being weak that had caused her temper to snap that way. Imagine! Her father, Tom Howard—weak? These Russians needed a lesson!

Tabitha went into her room and took off Ines' beautiful peach-colored gown. She folded the green lace shawl and laid it carefully across the foot of her bed. Then, going to the wardrobe, she took out her white cotton gown with the design of small green sprigs. It was unmistakably American, the best that New Bedford had to offer.

Then Tabitha looked at herself in the mirror. Ines had shown her how to pile her hair high on her head, with just a few curls cascading past her ears. Tabitha reached up and pulled out the hairpins one by one. Her hair fell like a red cape about her shoulders. She brushed out all the curls until her hair framed her face in natural waves.

"Hello, Tabitha," she whispered to her image, and smiled at herself.

She took a deep breath and left her pretty room. She walked down the corridor and back into the dining room. As Don Alvarado's guests saw her, they became silent, one by one.

Tabitha walked back to her place at the table. The two Alexeis stared, stood up, and waited for her to sit down.

"I don't think we've been introduced properly," she said to the elegant Russian noblemen in English. "My name is Tabitha Walker. I'm from New Bedford, Massachusetts. Perhaps you've heard of it? No? It's an American port, on the Atlantic."

Now the two Alexeis realized the extent of their own stupidity. They almost fell over each other in their rush to apologize to Tabitha. It was Alexei One, the baron's nephew, who succeeded in proposing a toast. "To Miss Tabitha Walker—a most unusual American!"

Tabitha laughed a triumphant little laugh. It had been a small battle—one Don Alvarado, Juan, and Baron von Wrangell at the head of the table had scarcely noticed. But she had won nevertheless, and the thought delighted her. She even forgave the two foolish Alexeis. "But you see, Alexei One," she said, laughing, "I am not unusual at all. I am just an ordinary American girl."

"You're wonderful," Alexei One replied, admiring Tabitha's simple dress and flowing hair. "And you are even more beautiful this way. After dinner, can we take a short stroll together?"

"Why would you want to stroll with an American? I'm liable to be too loud—or, worse yet, too plain. Everybody in the world knows that American girls don't know how to act."

Alexei Ubetskoy's eyes gleamed as he looked at

Tabitha. "I'll take my chances if you will. You think we have said some bad things about the Americans tonight? Then I will make up for it by saying wonderful things about you tomorrow."

Tabitha hesitated. She had no desire to go walking in the moonlight with Alexei Ubetskoy, yet perhaps he knew something more of the Russians' plans. Juan, with his talk of reading the enemy's mind while gazing into his eyes, had given her an idea.

"Well?" Alexei One was asking. "Are we going for a walk?"

"*Si,*" Tabitha replied, casting down her eyes so he could not see into them.

Beneath the open sky, Alexei's vision for the future grew as large as the huge California moon that was shining on them both. "Of course we would prefer California as Russian territory," Alexei said. "We have Alaska already. With California, we would control the length of North America's coast."

"But Don Alvarado says he wants California to be completely independent—"

"Don Alvarado is a dreamer," Alexei scoffed. "The baron has been talking to the Mexican government for months. Mexico could use a strong ally like Russia—it might be worth giving up California for that!"

"Give it up?" Tabitha was astounded. "This is a country, not a book or a pocket handkerchief!"

Alexei looked at Tabitha, and his eyes grew suddenly wary. "Perhaps I have said too much. Besides," he took Tabitha's hand, and tried to draw her closer to him, "why should I talk politics to such a very pretty American girl?"

Then he swept her into his big arms and tried to kiss her. Well, so much for all those fine European manners. She struggled in his arms, but that only made Alexei laugh and clasp her tighter.

"Let me go, you barnacle bilge!" she cried. It wasn't the saltiest phrase she knew, but it was close. She managed to get one arm free, and before Alexei could feel the touch of her lips against his, he felt a sharp sting across his cheek. Tabitha had slapped him.

He let go of Tabitha, and put a hand to his face. "A wildcat," he said in Spanish.

"An *American* wildcat," Tabitha replied hotly. "We call them bobcats—"

"That is right, that is what they're called here," Juan said, stepping out of the shadows. "They're small, but dangerous." He offered his arm to Tabitha. "Perhaps I should have warned you about them," he said to Alexei. "Only brave men dare to hunt them."

Alexei looked at Juan and Tabitha standing together and decided that he now understood why Tabitha had slapped him. "My apologies," he said clumsily. "I didn't know."

There isn't anything to know, Tabitha wanted to tell him. *Nothing to know about me and Juan, anyway.* But that, for the time being, would remain her secret.

"Shall we go in, Tabitha?" Juan asked her. "And have I told you how very pretty you look in that dress?"

He reached an arm around her shoulders in the darkness but Tabitha resisted him. "Will you take me inside now, Juan?" she asked.

She pressed her lips together at the absurd comedy of it all: Alexei trying to kiss her in the moonlight; Juan, convinced he was her *novio,* rushing to her defense; and, somewhere out there under the big California moon, Tom, convinced that she didn't care a fig for him. Only Tabitha knew the whole truth. Only Tabitha knew how desperately her heart hungered for Tom Howard.

Chapter 18

Don Alvarado had said the Russians were coming for dinner. But dinner, in the wide spaces of California, turned out to mean much more than that. The Russians stayed for two whole days at the Alvarado ranch—long enough for them to convince Don Alvarado to agree with their point of view. But Tabitha wasn't so sure that Don Alvarado was really convinced.

On the afternoon of the second day, she and Ines had just come onto the verandah, where the men were talking, carrying pitchers of cool lemonade. "And you'll finally be rid of the governor that Mexico sent you," Tabitha heard a smiling Baron von Wrangell say. Tabitha looked at Don Alvarado quickly and was relieved to see that suspicion was still in his eyes.

"Who will you send to replace him, Baron?" Don Alvarado asked.

"You shall be rid of governors entirely," Baron von Wrangell replied. "My country believes that a colony has a right to self-government."

Tabitha saw Don Alvarado wince at the word *col-*

ony, but when he spoke his voice was calm and unhurried. "What I wish to know, Baron von Wrangell, is this—if Mexico decides they will not give California to you, how are you going to make it your territory?"

Baron von Wrangell's smile became even broader. "It is a simple plan, *Señor* Alvarado," he explained. "Now that our course of action is set, we needn't wait for diplomatic decisions. No, we will act swiftly. The Mexican government, caught by surprise, will not oppose us."

"And what is it that you plan to do?" Juan Alvarado asked eagerly.

Tabitha poured lemonade into the men's glasses slowly. She did not want even the clink of the pitcher to keep her from hearing the baron's words.

"First," said the baron, "my men and I will march into Fort Ross and capture it by surprise. We will take down the Mexican flag that flies above the government building and raise the Russian flag in its place." He gave a short laugh. "We want no bloodshed and, besides, the Mexicans have no army in California to stop us. Then, my friend, we will move up the coast, raising our flag wherever we go. By the time the Mexican government learns of what we have done, it will be too late—all California will be ours."

"But what about the Americans?" Don Alvarado asked, voicing aloud the question that had formed in Tabitha's own mind. "There are many people here from the United States, and they hope that California will become a part of their own country."

"Let them hope," the baron laughed, and Tabitha's hand clenched tight on the handle of the pitcher. "By the time my men march into Bodega Bay and Fort Ross it will be too late for them to do anything about it. The American army is thousands of miles away—they are hardly a threat to us."

Blood beat in Tabitha's temples. She whirled back into the house and set the empty lemonade pitcher down with a crash. Baron von Wrangell would be marching on Fort Ross and she knew that Don Alvarado and the others would do nothing to stop him!

"Tabitha," Ines said, coming into the kitchen behind her. "Is anything wrong? Is it the heat? You look very pale."

"No, no," Tabitha said, cupping her hands under the kitchen pump and touching the cool water to her face. "I'm fine. I'll be back out in a minute, Ines."

Ines nodded and left the kitchen. *I have to do something,* Tabitha thought. *There are so many Americans at Fort Ross—I have to warn them somehow. I have to!*

But it wasn't just simple patriotism that moved Tabitha, and she knew it. It was also the idea that Tom Howard might still be at Fort Ross. And if he was, he would be in danger.

Tabitha had until the next day to put her plan into effect.

Her plan was a daring one, but she couldn't do anything about it until after the Russians had left the ranch. This time she would have to ride away from the Alvarado ranch alone.

But what would she do when she got to Fort Ross? Whom would she talk to? Who would believe her? Tom. He was her answer. She had to find Tom—not only to warn him but because she knew that, no matter what had passed between them, Tom would help her. She remembered with a pang the way Tom had ridden away from the Alvarado ranch—he hadn't even turned back to look at her, not even after she had called out to him.

But never mind all that now. She needed Tom's help and even if he was furious with her, he wouldn't turn her away. Or would he? For all her confidence, there was a nagging worm of worry and doubt eating away at her. Was she right or wrong about Tom? She'd find out soon enough—or at least as soon as she could get to Fort Ross.

Tabitha got up just as dawn was making its way across the sky. She put on the riding clothes that Ines had given her, and she tiptoed out of the house and to the stable.

Belleza gave a whinny of greeting, and Tabitha fed her two sugar lumps. She hoped that would keep Belleza calm while she saddled her. Tabitha had never saddled a horse before, but she had watched Domingo often enough, and she thought she knew how to do it.

The first time around, Belleza gave a little buck of dissatisfaction, and Tabitha saw that she had done something wrong. The girth that held the saddle in place—perhaps she had made it too tight. Tabitha loosened the girth, and fed Belleza some more sugar. Everything seemed to be all right. But she still had trouble mounting a horse without help.

"Oh, stand still, Belleza," Tabitha whispered, but the animal made a half turn whenever Tabitha tried to get her foot in the stirrup.

Tabitha looked about and found a water bucket. She turned the bucket upside down and, using it as a step, she managed to get her left foot into the stirrup and swung her leg over to the other side. There! She was in the saddle, and she felt pleased with herself.

Except—except—she had forgotten to open the stable door, and she couldn't open the darn thing sitting on Belleza. Moving gingerly, Tabitha dismounted, using her bucket-step once again. She opened the stable door and ran back to Belleza. Tabitha mounted again—it was a little easier the second time—and she rode out of the stable and onto the road that would take her to Fort Ross.

Tabitha realized that going riding by herself was not as easy as she had thought. Until now, she had always had someone riding with her. Belleza, she decided, was not a born leader—she preferred following another horse.

Tabitha's hands on the reins, her heels banging against Belleza's flanks—all this seemed a touch too timid to Belleza. The horse realized that Tabitha wasn't that sure of herself, and she took advantage of her rider's lack of confidence by ambling along and stopping to crop an especially sweet-looking mouthful of grass from time to time.

"At this rate we won't get to Fort Ross for a month of Sundays," Tabitha said out loud to Belleza. "We're going to have to make better time than this."

Sit up tall, Tabitha. Heels down, Tabitha. Hold those reins, Tabitha, don't let them just hang from your hands. Juan had been a good teacher, Tabitha decided, remembering his words.

She sat up straight, placed her feet properly in the stirrups, and got a firm grip on the reins. Belleza responded with a toss of her head, and began to trot in a proper manner. Tabitha tapped her flanks decisively with her heels, and Belleza moved into a canter.

"This is much more like it," Tabitha said to Belleza. "We've got to get to Fort Ross before someone misses us. It would be just like Juan to come riding after us, wouldn't it?"

Belleza shook her head and stretched out into a gallop. For one scary moment Tabitha was afraid that she might fall off the horse. But then she got into the rhythm of the ride, and she began to enjoy herself.

In a little while, Tabitha saw the buildings of Fort Ross before her, and she rode into the town. She had to find Tom, if he was still here. She knew it would be a good deal easier if she could get off Belleza, but where could she find a friendly hand to hold Belleza's head while she dismounted? She could try it without help, but she was afraid of making a fool of herself.

Tabitha rode along the main street of Fort Ross, trying to pretend that she knew exactly where she was going and what she was doing. She had only one idea as to where Tom might be. She hoped he was still there, and that he hadn't taken another berth on a boat to China.

Tabitha rode up to the store with the sign that said, *The Russian-American Company*. That was where she had seen Tom the last time she had ridden into Fort Ross, and she prayed that he was there now.

Tabitha reined up in front of the store, still sitting on Belleza's back because she was afraid to dismount. "Tom," she called out. "Tom Howard!"

No one came out of the store.

"Tom," she called again, "Tom Howard—you'd better get out here!"

A man stuck his head out the door and looked at Tabitha. Then he went back inside.

"You better get out there, Tom," Tabitha heard him say in a curious mixture of English, Spanish, and Russian. Then she caught the words "red-haired filly."

Her spine stiffened at being so described, but soon she heard a welcome sound—Tom's voice. "Red-haired—" he echoed.

Tom stepped out of the store, frowning. But when he saw Tabitha sitting on her horse, the frown turned into a grin. "I knew that *novio* of yours'd get tired of you sooner or later. What'd he do, Tabitha, throw you off the ranch?"

A trigger of relief went off deep within her. It was going to be all right. Things were going to be all right between them. But there would be time for that later. "That's not why I came," Tabitha said quickly.

"No? Then maybe you better get down from that horse and tell me just why you did come." He took another look at Tabitha, and his grin widened. "If you can get off your horse, that is."

"I can get down just fine—if you'll just give me a little help."

Tom laughed and took hold of the bridle. "This what you need?" he asked.

Tabitha swung one leg over and climbed down. She was tired from her sleepless night and from the early morning ride. Tom looked at her dusty boots, at her hat that had fallen back, and at her tangled hair. His grin faded as he said, "Looks like you moved pretty fast on your ride. Is something wrong, Tabitha?"

"Yes," she said. "I've got something important to tell you, Tom, and it has nothing to do with us." And she told him all that she had seen and heard at the Alvarado ranch during the past few days.

Tom whistled and shook his head when she had finished. "That's news, all right. But what can we do about it?"

"Tell the men on the American ships in Bodega Bay," she said. "They could stop the Russians if they got together—Baron von Wrangell said he doesn't want any bloodshed."

Tom looked at her in astonishment. "No bloodshed? This isn't a tea party, Tabitha. You must have heard wrong."

"No, no," she explained swiftly. "The tsar doesn't want to squander his men on California. He told the baron so himself. The baron can take California by force *only* if he keeps the men out of a real battle."

Tom looked at Tabitha carefully. "Who else knows that?" he asked.

"No one."

"So when the men here at Fort Ross and out in Bodega Bay see that baron and all of those Russians, they'll figure they mean to fight."

"Yes," Tabitha cried. "Yes. But all we have to do is call his bluff. Oh, Tom, we've got to warn everyone before it's too late. Baron von Wrangell is already on the march!"

"All right, all right," Tom agreed. "Just one thing I'm worried about—everybody out in Bodega Bay knows I jumped ship. They might not believe me. They might just try 'n' shoot me themselves. Sailors and captains don't look too kindly on ship jumpers, you know." A frown of worry creased Tabitha's forehead, but Tom laughed it away. "Never mind, Tabitha," he told her. "I'll take my chances, long as you're with me."

They stood on the dusty street looking at each other for no more than a minute, though it seemed like an hour to each of them. "We'd better hurry," Tabitha said at last.

"All right," Tom said. "Let me go to the livery stable and see about getting a horse for hire. You wait here, Tabitha—you think you can manage that little-bitty horse while I'm gone?"

"I got here, didn't I?" Tabitha said. Her words were angry ones, but her voice was warm and tender as a western breeze.

Chapter 19

TOM QUICKLY WARNED EVERYONE AT FORT ROSS who would listen of the Russians' intentions, then he saddled his livery stable mount and set out with Tabitha for Bodega Bay.

As soon as they were within sight of Bodega Bay, they saw that there were many sailing ships anchored there, and that most of the ships were American.

"Tom," Tabitha said, still worried about how Tom would be received, "let me go alone. I'll talk to the captains and tell them what's going on. You've done enough just bringing me here, and if you rode back to Fort Ross now—well, you'd be a whole lot safer there."

Tom glanced across at her. "You mean you're worried about what's going to happen to me?" he teased. "What would your *novio* say about that?"

Tabitha sat up straight in her saddle. "Juan and I were never engaged," she said, "except maybe in Juan's mind. Honestly, Tom, don't you know me any better than that?"

Tom laughed. "I guess I ought to have. Does that mean you're unattached again, Miss Walker?"

Tabitha tossed her red hair. "I don't think this is the time or the place to discuss that," she said. They had drawn close to Bodega Bay. "Are you going to turn back?" she asked.

Tom shook his head. "I came this far, I won't turn back now. Besides, I have to start reclaiming my reputation sometime, Tabitha."

Talking to the American captains of the merchant fleet was not as easy as Tabitha had supposed it would be.

Captain Tree of the *Blue Heron* out of Gloucester looked at them with a fair amount of suspicion. At first he ignored Tabitha and concentrated on Tom. "Who are you?" he asked. "And what kind of a wild story are you telling me?"

"I'm Tom Howard."

"From what ship?"

"The *White Swan* out of New Bedford."

"The *White Swan*—I passed her coming here from Hawaii. If you're with the *White Swan,* how come you aren't on her?" He stared at Tom. "Jumped ship did you? Left your captain short a man—why should I listen to the likes of you?"

"Because he's telling the truth," Tabitha said. "I'm Tabitha Walker—my father is captain of the *White Swan*. You've got to believe me."

"Your father's Jedediah Walker? Then what are you doing with this scallawag here? You should know better than to have anything to do with this man!"

"Please," Tabitha said, "that's not important right now. What is important is stopping the Russians before they move their men into Fort Ross and take over California."

Captain Tree shrugged. "I'm not sure that's our affair—let the Mexican government worry about those Russians."

"The Mexican government isn't going to do anything about the Russians," Tabitha pleaded. "That's just it. We're the only ones who can stop them!"

"All right," Captain Tree said, "tell me again and tell me slow. Just what do you think is happening here, and why do you think we should do something about it?"

Captain Tree listened more attentively as Tabitha told him about everything she had heard.

"I seem to remember hearing that them Russians tried this sometime before," Captain Tree said. "Before your time, missy—and almost before mine. Managed to stop them then—guess we can stop them now."

Tabitha breathed a sigh of relief. "Will you come with us to talk to the other American captains?"

"I'll come with *you,*" Captain Tree said. "Hate to be in the company of this runaway."

Captain Tree accompanied them as they went from ship to ship, and all the men they spoke to reacted much the way Captain Tree had.

"I'll get all the men from my ship who are able," one captain said, "and we'll go to Fort Ross . . . but as for you," he said to Tom Howard, "if this were the Navy you'd be in irons—"

"And court-martialed," Captain Tree agreed.

"If California ever gets to belong to anyone besides Mexico," another captain said, "it should become part of the United States—lots of Americans settling here, and more headed this way. Sure we'll come with you," he said to Tabitha.

A small army of men gathered, with Tabitha and Tom and Captain Tree leading the way. It was a motley group; there were no uniforms, and not many guns.

Captain Tree looked behind him at one point. "May not be so easy to stop those Russians—not if they're coming with any kind of army. I don't know, maybe there's a force up in Sitka, and they're going to march down here too."

"They don't have any real army up there," Tom said.

"How do you know?"

"Because I've been working for the Russian-American Company—I've heard the Russians talking."

"Baron von Wrangell has a few soldiers," Tabitha explained, "but most of his men are trappers from Alaska and the Aleutians. He's got orders not to lose any of the tsar's men. He only thinks he can do this because, when we see him, we'll be too scared to fight."

That ended all debates and arguments right there. "Scared?" one of the captains echoed in disgust. "Us? Good American men scared? What say, boys? Let's show 'em what we're made of, eh?"

The captains and sailors marched to Fort Ross, where the people of the settlement gathered to watch the strange parade. There was a beautiful, red-haired girl on a black horse, a tall, blond young man who wore sailor's clothes, and a brigade of seafaring men.

"We're here," Captain Tree said to Tabitha. "Now what?"

"Now we wait," Tabitha said, remembering the baron's conversation with Don Alvarado. "Baron von Wrangell plans to take us by surprise, but the surprise will be on him. It won't be long, now."

She was right. That very afternoon Baron von Wrangell was seen riding toward Fort Ross. Behind him rode a magnificently uniformed troop of Russian soldiers led by Alexei Ubetskoy, and behind them came a group of men dressed in heavy furs and large boots. Beside the baron rode a flag bearer carrying the Russian flag on which was pictured a two-headed eagle. The baron brought his men to a halt before the small stucco building that served as Fort Ross's City Hall.

The baron saw Tabitha and the men gathered around her in the small plaza that faced the City Hall. For a moment he was confused. Had Tabitha come from the Alvarado ranch with all these people to celebrate the Russian takeover of Fort Ross? He wanted to tell them that this was just the beginning—after Fort Ross, he and his men would move on to other isolated settlements. Soon the Russian flag would fly over all the government buildings up and down the California coast.

But then he saw one man raise a crudely built flagpole. The man raised it high, and Baron von Wrangell's eyes were filled with the red, white and blue colors of the flag of the United States.

Of course, the Baron thought, cursing his own stupidity. *The girl's an American.* In a swift flash, he realized how easily his careful plan had been undermined. Tabitha had overheard all his plans and had done something about them.

The baron looked behind him. He had his soldiers—there weren't many of them, but they were well-armed. They could fire into the crowd of people gathered around the red-haired American girl.

But the baron saw that the settlers of Fort Ross—Mexicans, Americans, even Russians—had all gathered on Tabitha's side. They faced the baron without uniforms or fancy arms, but without fear either. And courage, as the baron well knew, was a formidable opponent.

The baron remembered that he had promised the tsar that California would become Russian territory without any bloodshed. This was important, because if shots were fired and men were killed, the tsar sitting on his throne in far away St. Petersburg would send no additional troops to help the baron build an empire in California.

The baron knew that the tsar and all the ministers who surrounded him were shortsighted. California was rich beyond belief. Combined with the territory of Alaska which was already Russian, the tsar would have a territory well worth holding. But the tsar's decision was final, and he was too far away for the baron to plead his case.

The baron was a diplomat—he knew when he had been defeated, and he knew how to lose with dignity. He signaled the men behind him to stand fast, and he urged his horse forward until he stood looking at the people of Fort Ross and the seamen from Bodega Bay. He carefully avoided looking directly at Tabitha.

"My men and I are on the move," he said. "It was a most pleasant stay in your country. Good day." And with that, he turned and led his band in retreat. Only one of the company, the foolish Alexei Ubetskoy, whom Tabitha had called Alexei One, turned and looked back. His glance fell directly on Tabitha. He couldn't believe what he had just seen.

Chapter 20

IT HAD HAPPENED SO QUICKLY AND SO EASILY THAT the men from the American ships thought it was some kind of miracle.

"Never thought they'd give in so easily," Captain Tree said. "Thought we might hear the sound of a gun or two."

"I knew we could stop them," Tabitha said firmly, although trickles of sweat had begun behind her knees and in the hollows of her underarms.

"You *knew?*"

"Well, I knew we *had* to."

Captain Tree gave her a wintry smile—the only time Tabitha ever saw him smile—and said, "Well, I guess you're Jedediah Walker's daughter, all right. But you're a long way from home. Want to sail back to the States with me, missy? I'm bound for Gloucester, and we could get you to New Bedford from there."

Tabitha shook her head. "I'm waiting in California for my father. He'll stop for me on his way back from China."

Captain Tree looked at Tom Howard standing by

Tabitha's side. "Don't like to leave Jedediah Walker's daughter here with no protection."

"Don't worry about me," Tabitha told the captain. "I'm going back to the Alvarado ranch, if they'll still have me, and Tom's going to—" She paused, and it occurred to her that she had no idea what Tom planned to do.

Tom stepped into the conversation, speaking to Tabitha but loud enough for Captain Tree to hear. "I'm taking you to the Alvarado ranch—I want to make sure you'll be all right there. And then I'm finding me a ship—"

"A ship! But Tom—"

"I've got to do it, Tabitha," Tom said. "It's the only way I can make things right. I can't have people pointing at me for the rest of my life as the sailor who jumped ship and who should be in the brig, or in irons—"

Out of the corner of her eye, Tabitha saw Captain Tree nod approvingly at Tom's plan. Maybe there was hope for the youngster after all, his look seemed to say. Then, clenching his pipe between his teeth, he walked quietly away from them.

"I've got to make my name right in the seafaring world, Tabitha," Tom continued. He reached out for her, stroking her long hair with his fingers. "You see, I'm planning on asking a captain's daughter to marry me."

The words caught her off guard, exploding in her like kegs of gunpowder. Then she recovered herself and looked up into his sea-colored eyes. The smile that had first drawn her to him, that special smile filled with sunlight, was there. "A captain's daughter," Tabitha echoed. "Hmm. Is it anyone I know?"

"I don't know. Ever heard of a Captain Brisby of the *Scout?* Well, he's got a mighty pretty daughter, lives up Cape Cod way, an'—"

"Tom Howard," Tabitha said, "you're terrible!" But she was laughing, and his teasing only made her feel all the luckier to have fallen in love with him.

Tom grinned right back at her. "Well, I'd ask that Tabitha Walker, of New Bedford, but she seems to be engaged to some fellow named Juan."

"I told you," Tabitha said, "that was all a mistake."

"Oh?" Tom said, his eyebrows raising. "Well, what about your plans to see the world from the deck of a boat? What about going to China and all that? You mean you're willing to give all that up?"

"No," Tabitha said, shaking her head. "But my mother sailed with my father. I don't see any reason why I can't sail with you."

"Heaven have mercy on me," Tom said, laughing.

Tabitha planted her fists on her hips. "Now what is that supposed to mean?" she asked.

"It means I'm asking you to marry me, Tabitha, as soon as your father gets back from China. Why, if I spend the time working routes to and from Hawaii, I should have my first mate's papers by then. Think he'd like a first mate for a son-in-law?"

Tabitha flung her arms around his neck and kissed

him. "He'll have to," she said. "Otherwise there'll be a mutiny."

Tom returned Tabitha to the Alvarado ranch. It took all evening, but between the two of them they explained all that had happened. Don Alvarado was pleased that Baron von Wrangell had been stopped, and even Juan's opinion of Tom seemed to go up several notches.

Even so, Tabitha was not completely certain that Tom had been accepted until, after dinner, he was invited to spend the night. On the way upstairs to their rooms, Ines caught Tabitha by the arm. "It's that boy you saw in Fort Ross that day," she said. "You are going to marry him, no?"

"Yes," Tabitha answered truthfully, "I am. As soon as my father returns."

"I think," Ines said, her black eyes glowing, "I think you have loved him for a very long time, haven't you?"

"Yes, I guess I have." She smiled suddenly. "I had to sail halfway around the world to find it out, though."

For a fraction of a second Ines' beautiful face was downcast. "I am sailing nowhere," she said. It was the only time Tabitha had heard her express any sort of discontent.

"Then someone will sail to you, Ines. Someone who is just right for you."

Ines brightened. "Do you think it will happen that way?"

"I know it will," Tabitha replied. Her own happiness was so great that it ran out of her, splashing and tinting everything she came in contact with.

The next day was full of bittersweet beauty. Tabitha and Tom went riding—riding through the beautiful California countryside just as they had once planned to do.

"Tabitha," Tom said slowly, "are you all that dead set on sailing with me after we're married?"

Tabitha looked at him sharply. "I hope you're not starting to give me orders already, Tom," she replied. "Yes, I'm set on it. I told you long ago—there'll be no widow's walks for me."

Tom hesitated. "But what if there were something else?"

"Something like what?" she asked.

"Well, I was lying awake last night, thinking, and it just seemed so kind of beautiful and peaceful here, and I thought—well, Tabitha, what would you say to settling down on dry land? Right here in California?"

Tabitha's face brightened. "Oh, Tom!" she cried, so excited she almost dropped the reins. "I wouldn't mind *that* at all!"

Tom smiled. "I was hoping you'd feel that way. I'm still going to sail until your father comes back, though. I have to get my reputation back, and that way I can put some money aside for land and a house."

Tabitha tapped her heels suddenly against Belleza's sides. The little horse shot off, and Tom followed close behind.

"Crystal Springs," she said, when they reached the

clear pool. "The moment I saw this place, Tom, I wanted you to see it, too."

"Because of the flowers," Tom said. They're like the violets in New Bedford." He dismounted and helped Tabitha dismount, too.

Finally she was in his arms—in his arms with no one else to watch them. She felt his lips gently touching hers and she rested her head gently against his shoulder, wishing that she could stay there forever.

Tom knew how she felt because he felt the same way. But their future together was just beginning. There would be time enough to fulfill all the dreams and desires that were now in their minds.

Tom held her close, letting his lips wander along her smooth skin. "So what do you think, Tabitha? You think California's an adventurous enough place to settle down? You won't go getting bored on me, will you?"

Tabitha gazed up at him. "No, I don't think there's much danger in that. Not as long as you're here with me." She looked for a long moment into his eyes, then she kissed him. It was the right time, she thought. She could say it now. "Tom Howard," she said, "I love you. I mean to be your wife and never leave you."

She closed her eyes while he kissed her as slowly as he could. "Now that," he breathed softly, "is the most adventurous thing you've ever said."

Holding him in her arms, Tabitha suspected that he was right.

AFTERWORD
A Historical Note

An important part of this book is based upon a little-known incident in American history. Very few are aware that the Russians, led by Aleksander Baranov, traveled south from their territory of Alaska to California in the early part of the nineteenth century.

Recognizing that California was a rich hunting ground, the Russians established a community at Fort Ross—north of present-day San Francisco—near a river which is still known as Russian River.

At this time, California, along with Mexico, belonged to Spain. But Nicolai Rezanov, a minister of the tsar of Russia, had hoped to make California a Russian territory. Rezanov believed that he could create a Russian-American trading alliance, and that California would be a rich and important asset to the Russian Empire.

California, however, is a long distance from Russia, and the Russian government was not willing to commit a large amount of money or a grand army to the project. They were willing to accept California but, because they were too involved with pressing problems in Europe, they were not willing to fight for it.

Meanwhile, in 1810 the Mexicans had begun their fight against Spain for their independence, and in 1821 Mexico was proclaimed a republic. California then went from being a Spanish territory to a Mexican territory.

Promise Forever takes place in the 1840s—at a time when many different groups were looking at California with interest. The natives, who called themselves *Californios*, were mostly descendants of the original Spanish settlers. They had the idea that, just possibly, California could break away from Mexico and become an independent country. The Russians, led by Baron Ferdinand Petrovich von Wrangell, the first governor of Russia's Alaska territory, thought once again that California might become a Russian territory. The Mexicans, now that they had broken from Spain, seriously considered trading California to the Russians in the hope that they would gain a strong ally.

But Americans were moving westward. More and more people from the United States were settling in California, and many of them began to view California as a possible American territory.

Much of the activity carried on by all these interested groups was clandestine, and never went beyond the level of intrigue and semi-secret negotiations. Baron von Wrangell was the only one who thought of taking serious action at that time, but without real backing of money and men from his government, there was little he could do and, therefore, California did not become a battleground.

In 1846, as a result of border incidents between the United States and Mexico, the Mexican-American War began. The war ended in 1848 and California—as well as Arizona, Colorado, Nevada, Utah, and a large part of New Mexico—were ceded to the United States. California became a state in 1850. Alaska was sold by the Russians to the United States in 1867—much to the dismay of Baron von Wrangell, who recognized that the Russians had parted with a very important territory.

Other than Baron von Wrangell, the characters in *Promise Forever* are fictional, but they are based on people who lived at that time. American sailing ships did sail from New England to California and China, and there was a Russian-American Trading Company—John Jacob Astor, the founder of a great American fortune, was one of the principals of the company.

The Californios, with their Spanish and Mexican background, had a culture that was markedly different from that of the New Englanders, and the characters of Tabitha and Ines indicate the differences.

Dee Austin

If you would like to know more about the historical period covered in this book, the author suggests that you read the following books:

Chapman, C. E. *History of California: The Spanish Period.* New York: Gordian Press Inc., 1971.

Stackpole, Edouard. *The Sea-Hunters: The New England Whalemen.* Amherst: University of Massachusetts Press, 1953.

Is sixteen too young to feel the . . .

Dawn of Love

Romance, excitement, adventure—this is the combination that makes *Dawn of Love* books so special, that sets them apart from other romances.

Each book in this new series is a page-turning story set against the most tumultuous times in America's past—when the country was as fresh and independent as its daring, young sixteen-year-old heroines.

Dawn of Love is romance at its best, written to capture your interest and imagination, and guaranteed to sweep you into high adventure with love stories you will never forget.

Here is a glimpse of the first four *Dawn of Love* books.

#1 RECKLESS HEART
Dee Austin

The time is 1812, and wild and beautiful Azalee la Fontaine, the sixteen-year-old daughter of a wealthy New Orleans shipowner, is used to getting her own way. There's a war with England going on, and Azalee is warned to curb her reckless ways, but her daring and scandalous behavior makes her a prisoner in more ways than one. While the pirate captain Jean Lafitte can save her from one danger, only Johnny Trent—Azalee's fiery young man in blue—can tame her heart.

Read on . . .

#2 WILD PRAIRIE SKY
Cheri Michaels

The time is the 1840s; the place is the wagon trail west to Oregon. Headstrong Betsy Monroe knows she can meet any danger the trail offers. But Indians, raging rivers, and stampeding buffalo are the least of her worries. There's also Charlie Reynolds, the handsome young trail guide whose irresistible grin means nothing but trouble. When fate throws Betsy and Charlie together only two things can happen: all-out war or a love strong enough to shake the mountains.

#3 SAVAGE SPIRIT
Meg Cameron

The Kentucky frontier of 1780 is a wild place, as Catherine "Cat" Brant finds out when she is captured by Shawnee Indians and carried hundreds of miles from her home. Living in the Indians' village, she falls passionately in love with Blue Quail, a white captive who has been with the Shawnee so long he considers himself one of them. Can Cat make Blue Quail love her enough to leave the Indians and go back to her world?

#4 FEARLESS LOVE
Stephanie Andrews

It is hard to find time for romance during the 1836 Texan War for Independence from Mexico, but fiercely independent sixteen-year-old Lucy Bonner manages to share a few stolen minutes of love with Jesse Lee Powell, a crack young Tennessee rifleman. Lucy risks everything when she tries to save Jesse Lee and the other men of the Alamo and comes face-to-face with the Mexican Army and General Santa Anna himself!